DARKWHITE

Shweta Brijpuria

Leadstart
INKSTATE

ISBN: 978-93-83562-42-8
© Shweta Brijpuria, 2020

First published in India in 2013 by Frog Books
An imprint of Leadstart Publishing Pvt Ltd

Revised edition published in India in 2020 by
Leadstart
A division of One Point Six Technologies Pvt Ltd
Building J2, Shram Seva Premises, Offices: 119-123
Wadala Truck Terminus, Wadala (East)
Mumbai 400 037, Maharashtra, INDIA
T + 91 96 99933000   **E** info@leadstartcorp.com
W www.leadstartcorp.com

Disclaimer: The views expressed in this book are those of the Author and do not pertain to be held by the Publisher.

Cover Design: Mishta Roy & R. Maharajan
Layout: Logiciels Info Solutions Pvt. Ltd.

Dedication

My family
My friends
My teachers
My employers
Madhya Pradesh
The aspirations that build in millions of young hearts

About the Author

Shweta Brijpuria hails from the city of lakes - Bhopal. As a *didi* to her younger siblings, she grew up to be quite disciplined. She was scared of Math, but loved to write to the extent that even a difficult formula could be converted to couplets. She was close to her father, who instilled a fire in her to be different; he told her interesting stories about her great grandparents that inspired her to make a mark herself. 'Marketer by profession, but a poet at heart' is how she describes herself.

Having authored two novels, she has learnt to accept the challenges life throws at us with grace and courage. At first, it was hard to believe, but now she knows the stories of our lives are already written and we are merely playing our parts. The irony we are made to believe is that one has the liberty to navigate through their story at their own will, but that is where the conflicts begin and so does their story.

This realisation has made her fall in love with life and people more than she ever had before. She is all set to further explore life, writing and living; for there are no endings in a story, just beginnings of new chapters.

Acknowledgements

Journey to the Dark White would have been incomplete without you...

It was not easy, but you all made it possible for me. Mom, papa thanks for your never-ending love and support. Deepak, Saurabh, Chirag, my darling brothers, thanks for your love and encouragement. Vibhu, thanks for being my sister and not just Bhabhi. Niti, my darling little sister and a mother of shaitaan Pratham, thank you for knowing me more than myself.

Thank you Rohit my dear friend–you were the first one to visualize the scorpion gang live and here we are today. Dixit Uncle, your kind and encouraging words have been that driving force. This 'beti' of yours is thankful to you from the bottom of her heart. Soni Uncle, thank you for your guidance and your presence while taking the toughest decision of my life. Ashok Uncle, thanks a lot for your inputs; without them I would have never been able to connect the dots and discover the dark side of white. Kavita Aunty, thanks for being there and caring for me as your own daughter, I feel fortunate indeed. Medhavi Bhabhiji, thanks for all the encouragement and support all through, it helped me believe in my work.

Yash, thanks for being my coach and keeping a regular check on the progress. Thank you Yashika, Ruchi, Bela, Surekha, Pallavi and all my friends who have been a part of my journey. Thank you Anshuman, my Chotu Bhai, for playing such a crucial role at the last moment, it means a lot. Thanks to all my employers and bosses who have shown faith in me and believed in my marketing abilities. I am thankful to my teachers and professors who always encouraged me and my writing skills, my school and colleges. I am thankful to my publisher Leadstart, for putting their trust in me and without you this dream would have just been a dream. Thank you so much Snehil for making Dark White – Dark7White grand - it means a lot. Thank you, ALT Balaji and Zee, for putting your trust in the story and bringing all the characters to life. Thanks to the writers, actors and production team members for their efforts and making this project as yours. Thanks to CCD Amboli, Veera Desai staff and McDonalds Andheri staff for taking care of me, as I completed my book. The list is endless only to make me realize that I am lucky.

I know fortunate like me are few

With so many good people old and new

Just words are not enough to say 'Thank you'

All I am is only because of you.

Contents

Chapter 1

The Call of the Destiny

With sun, moon, stars and all planets besides,

in their folds together, my destiny resides.

What happens next, my Karma and they together will decide.

To know thy game, my heart is anxious from inside.

It was a dark night, and in the middle of dark trees, stood a big *Maa Durga* temple up in the mountains of Pahargarh, a small village in North Madhya Pradesh. It was over hundred years old and built by the Rajput family.

The son of the Rajput family, Keval Kishore Rajput, along with *poojari* of the temple, was offering prayers. They chanted with the objective of thanking Maa Durga for her blessings, and the victory that he achieved.

One needs to be thankful for all the things one has in life. Rajputs can be very arrogant and proud. But such rituals were made by their ancestors, to make them humble enough to thank the very cause of their existence.

The *Aarti* was offered in all the four directions, as God is omnipresent.

Keval took a big Rajput sword and offered *Bali* (Sacrifice) to *Maa Durga*.

Prasad was to be prepared from it, for *Brahmin Bhojan*, without which the *Maha Pooja* was incomplete. Brahmins are our facilitators;

they take charge of the rituals performed during the *pooja*. They have been the most respected class in our community, ever since it was categorized on the basis of the physical and mental strength that individuals possess.

"*Acharyaji,*" said Keval, and touched his feet. Rajput family had a lot of faith in him.

"*Rajputa putra aayushmaan bhava,*" said *Aacharyaji,* the head of the *Mandir* and their family *Guru.*

They believed that it was because of his blessings, that 25 years ago Keval managed to survive, when all the renowned doctors had given up hope.

Keval met with a very bad accident in Pahargarh, and there was no hope of his survival. *Acharyaji,* then performed *Maha Pooja* for Keval's life and he recovered.

Today *Acharyaji* performed this *Maha Pooja* for Keval's big victory. They kept looking at each other for some time; there was respect in Keval's eyes and an expression of content on *Acharyaji's* face. More than words, their eyes communicated with each other.

"*Hukum apkaa saamaan,*" came a servant with Keval's wallet, brief case, mobile phone, laptop and keys, breaking the silent communication. It was not their regular practice, but they were instructed to do so by Keval before the *Maha Pooja* started.

Keval Kishore opened the lock of his brief case, took out Fifty-one Thousand Rupees and looked at his mobile phone. There was no network yet. He touched feet of all the *Brahmins*, gave them *Dakshina,* and thanked them for their support in the *Maha Pooja.* "*Agya dejiye Acharyaji, jaldi hi aaunga.*"

"*Kintu Beta Pooja ke baad tumhe thodi der Maa Ke Darbaar me rehena chahiye, yeh zaroori hai, aur abhi prasaad bhi baki hai,*" said Acharyaji.

"*Acharyaji aap hain na hamari aur se, zara jaldi mein hun,*" replied Keval Kishore."*Apni zindagi ki raftaar par niyantran rakho beta.*

Tum samajhdaar ho. Khush rahoo. Ayushmaan bhava," said Acharyaji allowing him to leave, though he was not very happy with it.

Acharyaji was very old now. It was not easy for him to go down with Keval, even if he wanted to. *The Mandir* was his home and for generations his family has been there, as caretakers of *'Maa Durga'* idol, ever since Rajput's built this temple.

The temple was still in its original self, with no fancy architecture except for electricity; that was essential. Keval grew up seeing the same names inscribed on those mountain rocks. They say it was more than 200 years old. It was as if the place did not age, but Acharyaji did.

After taking leave from him, Keval immediately rushed down the stairs towards the car where his men were waiting. There were very few light poles, but only at the top. As they moved down the tenth step, they entered a dark zone. The men used mobile lights to make their way, but Keval swiftly jumped from one step to the other as if he could see in the dark.

It was his years of experience and attachment with this place. For him, this place was the source of energy.

"How do you manage Sir?" Asked Barman, his secretary.

"This is my home, Barman," Keval replied as he jumped down two steps at a time.

Mobile network was available there. As soon as he reached the car, Keval called his father to inform him about the *Maha Pooja*, *"Dau Sahab, pooja samapt ho gayi hai."*

He sounded tensed, "When are you leaving son?"

"Right away, *Dau Sahab*, I just called to inform you. How is *Maa Sahab*? Tomorrow is my first day in the CM office. We all are shifting to the CM House soon," he said to his father."She is fine, come as soon as you can son, we are waiting for you," said the proud father to his 33-year-old son.

"Driver jaldi chalo," Keval said and got into his car, occupying the back seat. His car followed the pilot car and behind it were four other cars with a team of three dozen men, all ready to leave with him.

The distance till Bhopal was to be covered in 9 hours by road. Pahargarh was a small village on the hills. The road was not very good. In fact, it was dangerous for a night journey. But nothing in this world was more important than Keval's next day.

Six cars were cutting through the darkness of the night, one after the other. It was as if this was a *Maha Yatra* after the *Maha Pooja*. The spiral road was not smooth. There were strange twists and turns, there were sign-boards with "Blind Turn" written on them. But the danger could not be sensed, unless met.

It wasn't a New-Moon night, yet there was no moon to be seen in the sky. It seemed to have gone to another world to welcome a new guest.

Patiently awaiting its move, danger welcomed men in the cars. Road became so narrow, that without even realizing, cars touched the edge, making drivers struggle, to make up for it. If the front car made one wrong move rest five behind would suffer.

Keval was alone with the driver. Mobile network was playing hide and seek. It was raining with no light but thunder. Though it was summer time, it seemed as if even nature wanted to break its law that day.

The driver was fully focused on his job, until he saw a truck moving at an uncontrollable speed, from the opposite direction, *"Ye zaroor marega sahib,"* said the driver. Keval did not respond, instead directed him to focus. The driver sighed with relief once the truck crossed them. As they went ahead, they saw that there was an accident. The driver of the van seemed to have lost his control and it hit the edge of the van from left side. Door of the van was shut but driver seemed to have been badly injured. There was not enough light to see if there was any one inside the van.

Keval wanted to stop and help, but he had to meet his deadline, so could not afford to waste even a single minute. He was soon to be Chief Minister of the State, how could he let anyone in his kingdom suffer in front of him.

It was time for him to be sensible and practical. He could not reach out to each and every person of his state himself, so he called his men in the last car to stop and help the victim.

"Hope he doesn't die," Keval said to himself, but the driver thought he was talking to him.

The driver replied, "*Sahib aap bahut ache hain.*" He did not feel like replying so just smiled with a little 'hmm' indicating to the driver that his words were heard. The driver understood. It was for the first time he was driving Keval's car. He was his mother's new driver, so was not quite aware of the 'Rajput traits'.

It was not an easy drive. In a split second they could see themselves touching the edge and felt as if they would be pulled down the hills, while the next second driver would take the first gear and climb up a steep road. It was like gambling with life, an attempt to commit suicide, which was technically not intended by any of those men in the cars, whose party leader had just tasted his first victory.

To further control the situation, Keval asked the driver to switch off the music. Surviving without music was impossible for Keval, and especially when there was nothing much he could do, but he did not want the music to end his song of life.

There was a torturing silence inside. One could hear only the screeching tyres of the cars. Rain had slowed down by now, but to add to the misery, the road was worse, and the night was pitch dark. There were a few lights in the dark, they were said to be the eyes of Jackals which shine in the night, making their presence prominent. Even if they were not barking Keval could hear them cry. Just as he was thinking about them, suddenly he saw a Jackal, as big as a dog walk down the road. 'He must have been on his hunt for a rabbit,' thought Keval.

The road patch worsened further. It was mud now, that was making it more difficult to drive; one could not even feel the edge anymore. Without any warning or invitation, the fall could now take the men in cars in its fold, bringing their life to an end.

The other side of the road was walled by a mountain, and there stood trees like demons. Some trees were straight and tall; they were pointed on the top. They seemed to be on their arrogant mission to challenge the sky, while others had ugly looking branches. Keval felt as if they were calling him to take him in their fold.

Keval knew these trees from his childhood; he used to wonder about their patience and the commitment with which they stood there for years together. But they gave him a different vibe as he was passing by.

It seemed like there was a landslide just before they arrived. Driver tried to be alert and took full charge of the difficult situation. Suddenly there was another small truck in the scene. This one crossed all the four cars which were behind and now was trying to overtake the first car.

Car driver honked, but the truck seemed to be in a hurry. Had there been a slight miscalculation all would have gone down. The car driver honked again and again, as if he was using some code language with the truck driver. He also blinked lights several times, indicating the irritation that the truck driver was creating. The truck driver gave a look, ignored the code, and moved on in haste.

"*Lagta hai hosh mein nahi chala rahe hain,*" said the driver.

"*Makhan Singh chup chaap chalao,*" said Keval. "*Sahib aap jaante nahi hain inn logon ko…,*" driver continued as he wanted to brag about his expertise in handling such men.

A "shhh" from Keval and the driver quietly got back to his work. The road ahead was smooth so the driver was relaxed. After a muddy patch the car tyres were happy, as they got to kiss a smooth road. They passed over the corn-sized pebbles without even letting the passenger get the hint of their presence.

They had already covered 60 kilometres till then, and it was clear that by no chance, would they be able to reach the capital in next 9 hours' time. The patch in the next 20 kilometres was smooth, though a little dangerous. But if they drove well, they could cover the few hours that they wasted.

Keval seemed to be a little worried about something all through the drive. The network was back so he made a few calls to the cars behind, all were in place but they wanted to halt for a while to attend nature's call.

Barman sitting in car number 3 called Keval, "Sir, can we stop somewhere?"

"In the next *dhaba*," said Keval.

Cars stopped one after the other, and the team ganged up next to Keval Kishore Rajput, as if they wanted to protect him from something.

They wanted to rush him inside the *dhaba*.

Since the rains were unalarmed and none of them had an umbrella, they tried to get some help from the owner, Jasvant Halwai.

"Jasvant Kaka, Sahab ke liye kuch ho to dena," said the driver of car no.3.

"Jo Hukum," happily Jasvant gave a long plastic sheet, as Keval left his car.

"Tees kadak chai kaka," again said the driver of car number 3.

"Tees Kadak," he shouted at the person in the master kitchen, and got something to eat for them.

An old man with a lantern walked inside the *dhaba*. He had also parked his bullock cart next to the cars. He looked equally proud of himself for some reason, as if even he had accomplished his mission. All men started looking at him, amused when he came in and sat next to them. He was not related to them in any manner.

"Malak log, aaj mausam bahut kharab hai, aap log yaheen ruk javo to theek hovee. Wo kutta bhi roo raha hai." said Jasvant Halwai to the driver of car no.4 as he looked at the bullock cart man, in amusement.

The men in white smiled at the old man, and ignored Jasvant's words. They moved out to leave, Keval sat next to the driver and they went off in their cars.

It was raining heavily as they left, but the road was smooth, so driver took off at a relatively high speed. It was 1:00 am already and suddenly a strong light appeared in front of them. The driver could not see clearly so honked loud. There was a honk of a truck, and the front car, at the same time in reply.

It seemed to be the same truck which had overtaken them on the rough patch sometime back. Looked like there was some problem with the truck and it had broken down in the middle of the road. The driver of car number one applied brake to slow down as a precaution.

Keval's driver tried to apply the brake, but to his utter horror the car would not stop. Brake had failed indicated the driver.

"It's impossible; it was fine when we stopped at the dhaba. Try again," said Keval.

They had reached very close to the first car and; driver tried hard to press the brake again and again, and turned the steering towards the left in the same speed. Before he could realize what he was doing, he lost control. Keval looked for his Asthma inhaler; it was in the side pocket. He got asthma problem from his mother's side, but it was not until two years back that he suffered his first attack. He tried to save his life.

Driver knew he had lost the ground, and now the wheels would rest only when they would land in *Ghati Gaon*. He was not sure if they would still be in the car.

His face started sweating profusely and he could not utter a single word. His hands started shivering and eyes rolled up, as if he had seen *Yamraj* right in front of him. And in the middle of this sequence, he suddenly started laughing, as if to announce his victory. The game of life was over.

"Oh no," screamed Keval and they were the last words uttered by him. The car disappeared in the dark and there was a sudden explosion.

The other four cars stopped, and out came the men with no words to say; no commands to follow. They were just trying to figure out what had actually transpired.

They were supposed to guard their party leader and the future Chief Minister of the state, but they had failed in their duty.

A quick action was important again. A few stayed there and rest went to the nearest police station, to inform the police.

The speed of the car was uncontrollable, the doors automatically opened and Keval was thrown out of his car, as if there was some third person inside, who was pushing him out. He felt weightless and could not fight any more. The man who practically was controlling the game of many lives for last ten years felt that he was failing to control the game of his own life.

He submitted himself to the hosts with a smile; he fell onto a branch of the same tree, which invited him on the way. It seemed as if the tree could move and had come to prove its potential to Keval. Trying to regain consciousness, Keval caught hold of a branch and moved up. But it was all wet. This made the grip difficult. The call of gravity was strong and the desire of trees below to take Keval Kishore Rajput into their arms was getting stronger. He lost control and slid down from one tree to the other. As if it was a game that was conspired against him.

In next three hours there were many people searching for Keval Kishore Rajput.

At 6:47 am in the morning men could hear the temple bell, the chirping birds, and felt a grave breeze. It was not raining, yet it was slippery. Even the sun did not show up. It was cloudy, though not dark, as if even the sun joined the moon.

They found Keval dangling 50 metres down the hill, on the branch of a tilted tree. He was all covered in blood, yet could be recognized easily. The body of driver could not be seen and people thought he must have died in the car explosion.

Everyone there thanked God for existence of the tree, which proved instrumental in saving Keval's life; otherwise tracing him down in the jungles below would have been like looking for a needle in a hay-stack.

25 years back, *Maa Durga* had saved his life, so everyone was sure of the miracle to happen again. He was the chosen one.

Three more men ran towards the tree for help to get him back. Ambulance was waiting above, along with the doctors. Media had also arrived. His father Mr Kishore Keval Rajput had come to take his son back.

As the expert team went to rescue Keval from the tree, and carefully bring him back, they realized that they needed to be very cautious. A tiny mistake or miscalculation could put him and them in the danger of falling down.

A team of seven people brought him up and rushed him into the ambulance. It took them around two hours to complete this operation. They had a hunch; something was wrong, gravely wrong. The team of doctors was ready for action.

As soon as he was laid on the stretcher in the ambulance, the doctor along with his assistants started his job. The moment they checked the heartbeat and tried to see the ECG, there was a straight line on the monitor; no heartbeats could be heard, neither any pulse could be felt. They were shocked, maybe excessive bleeding or a head injury or a trauma could have been the cause of his death.

It was difficult, but they informed the DIG police, that Mr Keval Kishore Rajput was dead. It was 9:30 am and he was supposed to be sworn in as the Chief Minister in the next half an hour, in the capital of the state, Bhopal. But as fate had something else in store for him, here he lay as a dead body on the stretcher of an ambulance.

They decided to take him to the hospital first, and then declare about his death to the awaiting media and the people.

His father had rushed to be at his son's side immediately, after he heard about the accident and was anxious to know his condition.

The Sun and the Moon had already taken him to the new world, even before the temple bell could carry Keval's message to Maa Durga.

The entire crowd that had gathered near the accident site followed the ambulance till the nearest hospital. The news was first broken to his father, Mr Kishore Keval Rajput, in the hospital. He was in a state of shock when he called his wife. By the time he broke the news to her, he took a massive heart attack. He was admitted in the ICCU.

The news of Keval's death came as a shock, for everybody present there.

Keval's mother reached the hospital from Bhopal in the evening. She rushed to see her husband first, who was showing no signs of recovery. The shock was so intense that he could not take it and died by middle of the night. Mrs Rajput was sitting in the hospital room with two dead bodies. She was shocked to the bones; she was almost numb with pain and agony. She was a very religious person, and was horrified at the sequence of events that had happened. Her whole world had come crashing down and was shattered into bits and pieces.

Since morning this incident was heavily broadcasted in all spectrums of media throughout the day.

It was a day of mourning for state which had lost its youngest, promising Chief Minister-to-be, and even more mournful for the Rajput family. The head of family and his son were dead and now survived by his wife, a four years old grandson who was legally adopted by Keval and Keval's fiancé Neelakshi Thakur, a renowned name in the PR industry.

The child resembled Keval, it was said that he was his own flesh and blood. This was a hush hush story in the corridors of politics; however, no one ever dared to speak about it aloud.

The last rites were performed the next day on their farm in Pahargarh, where a piece of land was reserved for this royal family. It was a tradition they followed, that the last rites of all their family members would be performed here.

Keval's adopted son gave the *Mukhagni,* and Acharyaji did the *pooja.* Acharyaji was feeling very guilty. He held himself responsible for both the deaths. He thought that he should have stopped Keval from taking up the journey so late in the night, or should have not given such a late time for Maha *Pooja.*

"Maa Durga kaise le sakti ho usko? Wo mere bête jaisa tha," cried Acharyaji as he continued the ceremony. It was not easy for him to come to terms with the fact that Keval was dead, when just one night before he had done *Maha Pooja* for him and blessed him with a long life.

The ceremony was done in the presence of all family members, including cousins who stayed in Pahargarh. More than a lakh of people had come from all over the state to pay him their last homage. Even women of the family were there.

Even after flames of the pyre went off, people did not go back, they continued standing there transfixed for a very long time wondering how such a young leader could pass away like this. Everything was silent.

Chapter 2

The Scorpios

I am born with a set of good and bad

Would have made all good, if another chance I had

For many things I do, I am called mad

Life has to be fun; it can't be sad. As piercing sun scorched the skin beneath her white cotton *kurta*, the soft breeze gave a sudden shiver and Neelakshi Thakur went deep into her thoughts. Neelakshi was so engrossed that she was unable to feel her own rolling tears.

He was her best friend who never believed in a relationship.

Down the memory lane she found a lot of reasons to smile and cherish, for whatever he gave was a treasure and whatever he took away from her was destiny.

Being a *Rajput* herself but from a different clan, they both had grown together as friends. Their families did not know about their friendship. They would always fight on petty issues and then make up again.

He had a dark side to him, but she never cared about its shade, because she was madly in love. She could have done anything for him.

She never realized her true feelings for him until he was leaving from Pune, leaving her with the Scorpio Gang. Today she found herself in the midst of a lot of questions, leading her to do a lot of soul searching.

*****

'Life until then was so carefree that I never had to think twice before doing anything, but it suddenly changed after I proposed to him. Was it a mistake?' She thought to herself.

*****

She was sitting in the balcony of her room, in the *Badi Haveli*, after returning from Keval's last rites.

As proud Ms Perfect, "The Charas" of her Scorpio college group, she was good with everything: her makeup, hair, dress, shoes, and other accessories. She was a perfectionist to the hilt. No one could ever find fault with her make-up or grooming or her impeccable English.

She was a Graduate in English Literature with a Diploma in PR. She had an MBA degree in Human Resource Management. She carried herself with a lot of grace and was sleek and slender. She had a body, which could let men's imaginations go wild.

Neelakshi was very emotional and proud of her vocabulary. She was a perfectionist. Her dream was to search for a Mr Perfect on her own. She was very clear about the fact that he would not be a chauvinist Rajput from her clan.

Rajputs, especially from her clan, had never learnt to respect women. Their aim in life was to get married to the prettiest of the women, use them to have babies and then fool around; keeping their wives sulking and suffering alone at home without any solace from any other corner.

She knew for sure that she was not ready to sulk all her life. She just wanted to break the family tradition and set herself free, live independent and breathe in freedom.

As the beautiful face with high cheek-bones, for which she was loved, bent to one side, absorbed in thoughts, her lovely expressive eyes that usually shone bright when she smiled; complemented her sadness today. She was looking at the tall trees, which was planted by Master Mind (Keval Kishore Rajput) of the Scorpio group when he was a child. But she did not smile as she looked at it. She just wanted to run back to the lovely past when she had smiled, laughed, enjoyed without any fear.

Back then she was so much in control of her life because she had a dream to fulfil. Today her life seemed to be without any aim. There was no dream that could motivate her to live.

'The Scorpio Gang' was a gang of seven Scorpios, born just one day after the other in the same year.

Neelakshi thought of her golden times as she gazed at the tree,

*****

'We were all 21 years old at that time when we joined college and became thick friends during the two years of MBA course. A few of us were friends from before, but that bond grew stronger during those years of fun.

True Scorpios, that's what we were, other's preferred to keep their distance from us. We were born intelligent and some people believed that we were dangerous because of our deep analytical skills. We never had any problems in accepting whatever people thought of us, as it brought us into the lime-light and we all basked in that attention.

We were a bunch of unpredictable people. No one could guess what prank we were up to at what time, that would get them into some trouble. So, we were left to our own desires.

Except for studies, we loved doing everything else. We were not really serious about things that youngsters of our age would be. For us to have a career, and to do a routine, banal job to earn our livelihood sounded cheap.

'It has to be very big else, it will not be', is what we thought. But what else, if not big, was beyond our imagination.

*****

A faint smile covered her face as she thought of all the Scorpios,

*****

'Keval Kishore Rajput, our Scorpio Master Mind, was born on 1at of November. He exhibited all the true qualities to be the leader of our group and, under his supervision, fun doubled and tripled, because he knew how to get the best out of us to make everything more exciting.

None of us were perfect for the world, but yet we had made a picture of being perfect in our own minds. 'You are what you believe' was our *Mantra* in life.

Practically we were bad at academics, really bad, though we were good in our subjects of interest, but unfortunately that is not what the practical world around us believed in doing.

Master Mind had all the traits of a double Scorpio. He had a magnetic personality, but at the same time he was a bit secretive about his plans. His smart square face had a 'don't mess with me attitude' and a serious 'you can trust me' look in his eyes. His big forehead and jet-black hair, steel jaws made him look super cool to girls and intimidated the guys.

He wasn't very tall, but had a personality that was good enough to make him stand out in the crowd. He was always dressed in formal but did all the non-formal stuff that one could not even think of. His smart glasses added charisma to his personality. He was the darling of our group. He came from a rich family background. He was a Rajput from Pahargarh and had a big family business but never boasted about anything.

He could have chosen any premier educational institute in the world to do his Business-training course, but he did not go, or to be precise he was not sent by his father, to any such institute. It was believed that Mr Kishore Keval Rajput, Master Mind's father, had doubts about his son's capability as a businessman.

This made Master Mind a little difficult person; he would always be on the mission to prove himself as a better businessman than both his father and his grandfather, against all odds.

Every first Saturday of the month, ever since we were eighteen, he would wait for his father's call and the moment he called, Master would immediately rush somewhere and would not turn back till Sunday evening; he would come back frustrated, but would not utter a word.

Master was always organized and punctual in everything he did. He did his Honours in Political Science and had Economics as his second subject.

Nothing ever affected our friendship, neither his intelligence, nor the differences that he had with his father.'

*****

Neelakshi smiled as she thought of the next member of the Scorpio group;

*****

The Second one was 'Scorpio Dabbu,' Karan Kataria. He was born on 2nd of November.

He was an idiot and a real freak. Dabbu loved sports and travelling. He enjoyed talking a lot. He was a football player and, since childhood, used to play for the MP state team. He was a diehard fan of team Manchester United. Our group was his third love after the first two. He was a completely confused person, yet his pointed nose gave him a matured look. Once a person got to know him, you could make out that he was crazy in true sense.

This fun-loving handsome tall guy with a charming smile was our darling, and we loved to spend our time with him. He was regular in the gym and his physique would announce that.

His brown hair was always kept long, for he knew that he looked even more charming when those few strands of hair fell in front of his forehead and touched his eyes. They were always ruffled and looked too sexy. The kind of hair you would like to touch, play and ruffle them a little more.

He cracked jokes and laughed wholeheartedly, which made everything super cool and funny. He was quite revengeful though, which is a common trait in Scorpios.

In achievements, he was nowhere close to his father. At this age, his father had already started his business. He led the Republic Day Parade at Lal Parade Ground in Delhi, twice in his life, representing the Navy wing of NCC. He was the President in his college and wanted to be in active politics, for he had been under the guidance of his guru Dr Qureshi, but due to family responsibilities and a bad experience in politics he gave it up.

Moreover, he believed that at present politics was not the way it was in the good old days, when people had high moral values and were ready to die for the nation. At present it had become like a pyramid of power-hungry people. The significance of politics was different now. It was all a game of power, money and corruption.

'The third was 'Scorpio Shark', aka Raj Bhandari, born on 3rd November. He was full on *Jugadu*; if the word "*Jugaad*" had come into existence it was only because of him. He would get his work done either by hook or by crook. He had connections everywhere, and we managed to pass in most of our exams only because of him. During college festivals he would arrange for the maximum sponsors through his sources.

Bhopali Bataule seemed as if were originated from him. He could go to any extent to exaggerate things. He was clever and always knew how to turn the table in his favour. He was a good negotiator and represented his Marwari community really well.

Shark was an expert liar and was a habitual one; he could carry off a lie with great ease. His steel-grey eyes well complemented his traits.

He was inspired by cars and would always remember people by their cars. He had a small face, wheatish complexion, and his features were very sharp. His average height made him more inclined toward wearing boots with high heels, despite being laughed at for them.

As he was a good singer all his nonsense was forgiven once he would start singing the best of Kishore Kumar, Mohammad Rafi and Sonu Nigam songs. People could never forget him once they met him. He was a Commerce graduate from one of the most notorious college of the town 'BSSA' and was doing his MBA in Marketing with us.

*****

Neelakshi came out of her pool of thoughts for a while, rubbed her eyes and went back to the memories,

*****

'The fourth was me 'Scorpio Charas' an addiction, as they called, born on 4th November. There is nothing more than that word, she could think of to describe herself.'

*****

She thought of how fashionable she was. She could carry off everything she wore with great elegance. She would always save money to buy the trendiest stuff available in the market. She would not mind even stealing money from her father's wallet.

As she smiled and moved ahead to the fifth one, she thought of 'Scorpio Shady' the entertainer of the group.

*****

'He was the tallest of all and 'the stage man'. He looked super serious, but with his communication skill, he was capable enough of turning the entire parliament session into a plaything and with his theatrics, he would have people in splits. And mind you, his jokes were hard-hitting. He made sure he was taken seriously.

He could put any man to shame without even making him realize what he said. His oval shaped face with small eyes made him look very attractive, and the two horizontal lines on his forehead made him super-super cute. He always preferred keeping a ponytail and, while cracking jokes, he would run his hands through it. This would be an indication that he was now up to some mischief.

Shady would always get *jhaad* (scolding) from his mother for it. There was a strange tension between him and his parents, which others could never figure out.

It's a well-known fact that a person who is very unhappy makes you laugh the most. His fight against his inner sadness made him a Master of creating reasons to make others smile.

It was his sadness that motivated him not to share it with others, as it might rub on them. He tried his level best to make the lives of other people more comfortable and easier. He was the kind of person who would always lend his shoulder to people to cry on.

Spending time with him would mean that all our worries had to leave, making us feel extremely light-hearted. Here was a person who could have been a very good priest in the church where people could wash away their sins by making confessions.

Shady would never let us know about his tensions, and we respected him for that. We gave him his required space and made it very clear that whenever he needed us, we would go to any lengths to be by his side.

He was a confused person. He always wore white as it made others feel that he was at peace, though it was only an assumption on our part.

Very few of his friends were aware of the fact that he never wore a cap, as he had big ears which made him look like a monkey. To avoid being the butt of jokes amongst his classmates and others, he avoided wearing the cap as it brought undue attention towards his ears.

He never wore a half sleeve shirt either, because he was under a notion that girls did not like thin arms and he had thin ones. He tried to hide his weaknesses by his great sense of humour. He always wanted to be the centre of attraction in a gathering.

One would just want to listen to Shady and never leave his side. He was a darling of the group.

He did his BA (Honours) in Psychology because he loved to read people and had joined MBA in Marketing only to please his parents.

*****

Neelakshi smiled as she moved on to the sixth Scorpio.

*****

'He would finance most of our *mastis* but not for free, we had to pay him that money back with 1% interest the next month and if delayed he would increase the interest by 0.5% as penalty. This worked wonders for him and us, for him because it made him rich and for us because we were always on our toes to pay it on time.

We always felt it was too greedy of our *Bangali Pandit*; Shashank Sen Sharma 'Scorpio Bank' born on 6th of November, but yes it kept us away from over-spending. Just the thought of getting into debt, much before we earned was very scary.

Shashank Sen Sharma, our '*chirkut*', was very intelligent and looked extremely funny with a round face, big cheeks and small lips. His hair was unkempt and untidy which gave him a school boy look and he at times looked like 'Dennis the Menace.' He was too sharp at calculations; he wore funny square glasses and was used to biting his nails when he was tense or nervous.

He looked good with his fair complexion and athlete's body, but would always try to hide his good looks for some reason. He never wanted to come out as a person who had money. That was strange of him, but that is how he was.

He was one rich person who loved to portray himself as poor. He did his Economics Honours from Delhi and wanted to pursue his MS from US but since that needed one more year of education; he decided to do a full time MBA in Finance from a local college. This would give him enough time with his family, as he never intended to come back once gone. He was a focused person.

The seventh one was the loudest and the cutest member of the gang; she was a pain in neck at times, but an adorable girl. She was 'Scorpio *Sach Ka Saamna'*, Greshma Rastogi. She was my best friend.

Gresh looked extremely beautiful, with her curly brown hair, which she preferred to keep short. She had brown and shiny doe eyes, lovely skin and a charming smile.

I could never be jealous of her beauty, because she was a very affectionate and a happy-go-lucky girl. She was very naïve, emotional and caring. In college we were like Siamese twins, never seen without each other. More than half the boys in the college were crazy about her, but I would never let her know that, not that she would have ever cared. However, it would have made a big difference to me.

Our fathers were best friends since childhood and she was also a *Rajput*. Sometimes I felt sorry for her because I knew she would end up getting married to a *Rajput* and lead the pitiable life that I was running away from.'

*****

Neelakshi smiled as she thought of her friendship with Greshma and the way it strengthened as the years rolled by, unlike their father's friendship that often suffered a setback because of their inflated egos. Never in life did she stop thinking about her.

'Since school, Gresh was inspired by Kit Coleman, the first war reporter who covered the Spanish American war for *The Toronto Mail* in 1898. She was impressed by this fearless woman and had come across her in one of the kid magazines, when we were in school. Inspired by her; Gresh used to love reading news in the morning school assembly; something that kids of our age hated the most. She was different and mysterious in her own way. She had this strange habit of being honest, which forced us to drop her from most of our *plans* without informing her. She was under strict vigilance of our expert Scorpio friends to help her learn how to lie when it was important. She did try her level best, but somehow was very clumsy and could not develop this skill at the required rate.

When I did my diploma in PR, Gresh did her full-time Journalism course from Makhan Lal Chaturvedi University and then joined MBA in Human Resource.

Her father was about to get her married, immediately after graduation, but somehow as per her horoscope that was not the appropriate time. A family astrologer had raised an objection that there was some *Rahu-Ketu* issue. They are supposed to be strong planets which give direction to a person's action. Her parents believed in them far more than the capabilities of their very own biological daughter.

Her father had agreed to let her pursue her MBA studies with me, but made one thing very clear that as soon as she would complete it, she would get married. None of us knew that deep inside her heart, the thought of rebelling had already germinated. She wanted to be acknowledged as an intelligent person.

There was a fear that her mother had instilled in her mind, since she was a child and that was a major reason why she always kept herself away from guys. Even while talking to them, she made sure that she made no eye contact with them.

That fear became stronger as she grew up. She was paranoid of being raped.

Both of us never shared the secret of her being paranoid of being raped with anyone; as we were not sure how the others would react to it. A typical Scorpio trait!

Gresh never stayed away from home for long, nor did she ever go for school picnics. Funniest part was that despite being talented, she never participated in extracurricular activities. Even if there were extra classes in the school, which was not very far from her home. Her brothers waited for her till she finished and then would bring her back with them.

In the beginning, she was not comfortable with the boys of Scorpio Group, however later she realized that they were good, and it would be better and safer in a group where there would be boys to protect her, than running away from everyone. As I was a part of the group too, she developed a comfort zone and became friends with all of us.

We knew each other extremely well, as Scorpios and as individuals; still we kept a lot of things to ourselves and mentioned them only when it became necessary. For all of us, the most important thing was that we were having a great time together.

On the very first day of our college we got to know about each other's birth dates as the roll numbers were as per our dates of birth, unlike other colleges, where the names were arranged in the alphabetical order. Lot of students made fun of our birth dates initially, and we were surprised at the mystery too.

We were inquisitive and, with a bit of research work, came to know that nine months before our birth, there was a three-day curfew in the city, so our parents did the most sensible thing that a couple would do and brought us into this world.'

*****

This was too weird a thought to Neelakshi who, it seemed, had no control over her them. Thoughts have wings. They fly according to their own free will.

Mystery of their birth was first assignment given to the MBA batch they were in. This was their intelligent professor's idea to get all the students together. Four of them were amongst the last rankers in entrance exams while Keval Kishore Rajput (Master Mind), Karan Kataria (Dabbu) and Shashank Sen Sharma (Bank) were amongst the top rankers.

Chapter 3

The Search

I don't want to accept a few things about others and me

For perfect could be perfect but I am happy as are we

As rule breakers, as game crackers in this world we are born to be free

Rajput family servant came with Neelakshi's cell phone and informed that Maa Sahab had asked him to hand it over to her.

Maa Sahab is Master Mind's (Keval Kishore Rajput) mother, she belonged to the *Rajgharana* of Jaipur and it is said that Ramu Kaka had come as a part of her dowry, along with a lot of gold, cash, cattle and cars. He was her care-taker since she was a child.

Maa Sahab is 52 now, yet her skin was lovely; she showed not a single wrinkle on her face even if one took a closer look. She had a family history of asthma but thankfully was in the pink of her health.

She knew her son was a complicated person when it came to relationships, just like his father. She would work hard to strike a balance between both father and son, but despite her efforts the ego clashes between the two were unavoidable.

Her husband used to believe in the theory of spare the rod and spoil the child. He was a strict disciplinarian. Keval on the other hand loved him a lot, yet was always busy making plans to prove himself one up on his father and grandfather. He grew up with a good exposure to the business world and thus was very analytical.

Keval Kishore Rajput's father, Kishore Keval Rajput, was an extremely good businessman. At a very young age he took his grandfather's business to great heights, taking advantage of the economic liberalization and flexible government policies during that time.

He never believed in going out of his way and building relations with government bureaucrats or politicians. He had good business connections and was a smart worker.

He was an excellent orator and had in-depth knowledge of business, economics and *Bhagvat Gita* as well. He was '*Karma Pradhan*'.

As Neelakshi took her phone from Ramu Kaka, he bowed and requested her to get inside the room, as the sun would be harsh in the afternoon and she might suffer a sun-stroke. Summer afternoons were extremely bad in Pahargarh. She respected him, paid heed to what he said, and moved into her room.

She asked, "*Maa Sahab kaisi hain Ramu Kaka, aur kya Chote Kishore so gaye hain?*"

"*Hukum Chote Kishore Maa Sahab ke saath khel rahe the, abhi thodi der pehele inspector sahab aakar gaye hain. Aap ko kuch chahiye hai to bata dijiyega,*" he replied.

"*Nahi Kaka,*" said Neelakshi and looked into her mobile phone. There were many missed calls from office, close friends and media. She knew her friends wanted to be with her in this difficult time; however, she wanted to be left alone.

There was a big mess in her life already. Many things were spoken about her and Keval; she never understood the intensity of their relationship. She was struggling to find that out herself.

Ramu Kaka left the room with her sitting on a sofa next to the huge double bed. This used to be her room six years back; actually, Keval and hers. She again went back to remembering her old days at college,

*****

'The best time we spent was in the college backyard where Scorpio boys grew weed. No one in our families had the faintest idea of our adventures. Bhopali boys are notorious; they would do all sorts of *masti* and yet, could carry their pretence of being simple.

The girls were punctual; they reached home before the deadline of 7:00 pm set by their parents. We were very different from the usual girls. We were no less than boys when it came to having fun. Thank God, we were never caught, otherwise our fathers, without a doubt, would have committed suicide.

This was the first secret Scorpio boys shared with us and soon it became our secret too. It was the secret of *Charas* (and Ganja) after which I got my name 'Scorpio Charas'. It was the first time I had experienced it. And, yes, the feeling was irresistible, I loved the high. It was so difficult to accept this new discovery about myself. I could have been a potential addict in the making.

We don't realize, but if we watch closely, the five elements of life are static only because they want us to believe in our existence. The only element that is allowed to change is the sixth one, and that is 'time'.

Its responsibility is to make us realize that we have to move on to the next performance. The discovery of *Charas* in the static campus of our college, made me realize that the next action was to plunge into the undiscovered feeling.

The weed adventure was an outcome of expert research done by Mr Karan Kataria "Scorpio Dabbu". He learnt this skill from his visit to Mawna, a small town in Himanchal Pradesh. We did not know it could be grown so easily. There were rumours that it was smuggled from the backyards of some wealthy people.

We actually tried making it our self. We took out juice from the grass, poured it in a big plate and left it to dry so that the liquid could evaporate. The dried cake was crushed into a powder. This powder was sold for over three grands in the black market and was actually available to us for free. We could also sell and make money out of it. But we did not do that.

We took the dried powder, got a good brand cigarette and emptied the inside of it. We filled the powder into it and made an attempt to reach heaven.'

*****

Neelakshi smiled as she thought about that time, tried to stretch herself to relax her tired limbs and come out of the lethargy she was feeling because of skipping her regular gym. She went back to her pool of thoughts again,

*****

'During these two years our Bank (Shashank Sen Sharma) lost his heart to Gresh and it was now time for his '*Sach ka saamna*'.

While our little girl was absolutely disinterested in him, or anybody else for that matter, she did not pay much attention to the signals he gave. She knew it would never be an inter-caste marriage for her. And the bonus time that was given by her horoscope experts was soon to end.

Deep inside her heart Gresh was praying that her stars, which were supposed to be occupying all wrong places of her horoscope, would allow one more year of freedom to her. In that time, she could at least make an attempt to become independent and know what freedom actually meant.'

*****

The memories of those days were still fresh in her mind; she vividly remembered the scene created by Greshma when 'Scorpio Bank', Bangali Pandit - Shashank Sen Sharma, proposed to her.

*****

'Gresh was dumbstruck and then all of a sudden she showed her '*Rudra Avtar*'. She was furious and insulted the poor guy beyond words. Bank was shocked to the bones. It was just a proposal; she could have politely refused to it.

He got annoyed and the conversation that was supposed to be 'just between the two of them' had now become the talk of the entire college. It made an interesting case study for the management students around.

Everyone let their imaginations go wild; they were busy analyzing the situation and giving their expert opinions. 'Link up' is the best source of entertainment for empty minds and has been so since ages, even before the invention of cinema and television.

Gresh was not capable of handling this kind of unwanted attention; a girl who had always been running away from such controversies was now caught in the web. She over-reacted and spoilt everything, even the friendship.

Bank was hurt by her behaviour. With a mix of emotions in his voice, yet maintaining his dignity, he spoke to her in front of the crowd where he felt humiliated; "Greshma, you have to pay for it."

These guys have such inflated egos that could be compared to nothing else in the world; I wonder why these guys are so full of themselves. It is amazing to know from where they get such alarming words and the guts to spell them in one go.

Yes, even he had over-reacted. At least he could have been a little sensible. Gresh was already a handful.

I was really happy to see Gresh replying so confidently to a male chauvinist pig; it was for the first time in her life that she had made such a brave attempt. It seemed as if she was getting out of her cocoon, or at least making an attempt to get out of it.

Gresh gathered all her courage and replied back to him, looking into his eyes, "*Dost* let's see who pays for it in the end." Though it was a different story that she started shivering as she replied, but it was only me who could make that out.

*****

As Neelakshi thought about the conversation between Shashank and Greshma in the canteen eleven years back, her cell phone rang. To her surprise it was Shashank who had called her up.

Think of the devil and he is here, she said to herself and received the call.

"What are you doing Neelu?"

"Nothing, Shashank, I was just thinking of our old days and happy days. God knows where they are gone," she paused and continued, "I was just trying to turn back the pages of life, to see if I could get a few answers. But in the process, I am totally confused."

Shashank tried to distract her, "After such a long time you have taken a break, especially after that stupid Suparna body-wash scandal which goofed up the whole PR campaign, because of the incorrect information given by your client."

Neelakshi replied in a heavy voice, "Shashank please this is not a leisure break, my life has lost all its charm without Keval. He was everything to me and you know that. How can you even think of saying something so silly?"

"Neelu, please don't misunderstand me. It's a loss for all of us. What I meant was about your health, which is the biggest priority.

There are clients from abroad who have shown interest in investing in your agency, impressed by the rich client base that you have created against all the odds.

And it's for the first time that you are not available for such an important meeting. So, what else do you think should I say? It is a break from work. Right, and you know it very well that I did not mean to hurt you." "Yes Shashank, I understand, I am not available for this important meeting. But you can tell me when to come, I will be there."

"No need Neelu, everything will be taken care of, so don't worry. I have postponed this meeting to next week. And please, don't mind, but Gresh has already left to be with you and she would not be coming as a media person but as your friend."

"Please Shashank why? You know I want to handle everything myself? I don't need anyone; moreover, you know what Gresh would make out of it."

"Shut up Neelu, you need someone to take care of you and I don't want to listen to anything. Hope you are taking care of Maa Sahab and Little Kishore. Take care of yourself too," he said and disconnected.

This reminds Neelakshi that she had to meet Maa Sahab and is also supposed to check if Little Kishore was all right. She used to meet him only during her Bhopal visits. He was a small baby when she handed over his responsibility to Keval Kishore Rajput.

He performed the last rites of his father and his grandfather. He did not understand what he was made to do. Maa Sahab had insisted on it and no one could disobey her.

Neelakshi rushed into her room and said, "Maa Sahab", as there was practically nothing to say. Looking at her white sari she felt like crying aloud for the lady who would always be in rich, colourful designer *chiffon saris* with hand crafted *jadau jewellery* and matching footwear, but today she was mourning for her dead husband and dead son.

Maa Sahab never used to talk much. She was always known for her action and liberal thoughts, but at that moment she could not stop herself from saying, "*Beta,* I can understand your plight. I lost my husband, who was with me ever since I knew him. He gave me all the happiness of life, a lovely son, a beautiful life and respect. I wore *sindoor* and *mangalsutra* for thirty-four years of my married life. You are mourning for someone who gave you nothing."

"Maa Sahab please don't say that, whatever Keval was he was mine and whatever he gave to me, he gave to no one else. That is enough for me. He can't be wrong," replied Neelakshi and kept quiet as she had high regards for her.

It was a bonding time for two grieving women, who practically were in a relation without being in one. Neelakshi's mother and father had already disowned her years back.

"Police had come to verify some facts about Keval's death, Neelakshi. They are suspecting it to be a murder," said Maa Sahab.

"What are you saying, Maa Sahab? Who had the guts to kill Keval?" said Neelakshi with fire in her eyes that burnt strong as tears rolled down her eyes.

"They are only suspecting Neelakshi, as there is no evidence and they have not even declared it to media. For the rest of the world it is only an accident case, while there will be a team that will be going into the depth of this case till something strong comes out."

"What do you think, Maa Sahab?"

"For me I have lost everything and don't have a reason to look back but there is a reason to move ahead and that is my grandson," she said and became quiet, thus indicating that she wanted to be alone.

Chapter 4

A Smart Plan

Some things that rules can't define

Some things that you can't further refine

The sharpness of mind is such a divine

It could bring change even in a ravine

Post lunch Neelakshi took Little Kishore to sleep. He was quiet that day. It seemed as if he had many questions in mind and was struggling for answers. He was in a tender age that did not allow him to phrase those questions. He was quiet all the while. And soon he was off to sleep. It was 2:00 pm by then, the time seemed to have stopped for Neelakshi, but practically it did not.

If there were a scope to save time in the bank locker or to invest it somewhere for more returns, she would have filled all her bank accounts and lockers with time in exchange for all the wealth she had. In the hustle bustle of super occupied life, one doesn't know when and where time flies.

It is so important for a person to be occupied with something constructive to make best use of time. It controls the most vulnerable part of you, your mind. Neelakshi had time today but no control over her mind. It was curious and curious for many answers; she could construct her questions unlike the little boy but could not find anyone to answer them. She found her life heading nowhere. The worst and best part of life is that nothing is permanent, as time never allows it to be. But we keep struggling trying to strike a balance all through, within our self. We keep on fighting till the end without realizing that this balance of nature could be managed only from deep within. The same within which is occupied in resolving the complications that we create. Even Neelakshi failed to understand this truth.

She started connecting with the old time again,

*****

'Dabbu (Karan Kataria), the sports freak, tried to control the situation post Gresh–Shashank issue by diverting everybody's mind to something serious, "Guys time please, there is no need to fight over love now, there is still time for it, we have our final semester exams soon" once said this, the crowd started clearing up and we got on to our serious group mission.

"The paper needs to be out well in time," he said when it was just the Scorpios together.

"Last time those two liquor bottles worked for us, *chaprasi ko pilaya*, so he gave us two papers and I got only six paperbacks instead of eight, but now the time has come to wash all my sins."

Dabbu's family is *kattar Brahmin*, no one drinks or eats non-vegetarian food; by mistake, his grandfather once ate an egg when he was young. He was made to offer a gold coin to the Temple *Poojari*, as punishment. This was how conservative the family was.

So instead of getting into any kind of monetary loss, that would only make the *poojari* richer. He chose to do his deeds in the dark.

Dabbu's father ensured that his son made best use of all his political connections.

Except studies Dabbu enjoyed everything else. He believed that stealing papers was not a big thing. Every proud student who aspires to become successful does it at least once in his lifetime. If not, then there was something seriously wrong with his aspirations. According to Dabbu, the rank holders are insecure people, and do not have the guts to dare. So, they choose the shortcuts of mugging up and retaining useless lessons, just to save their position in the race towards a blind future. These lessons, according to him, practically had no value after the exams.

He believed that the two most expensive things in the world, your time and space of mind, need to be used for better things in life. They are wasted by putting logics and energies into reproducing already discovered things on a piece of paper by lakhs of students, just to prove that one is aware of their existence. 'It would be better if so, much is invested in doing something more creative,' he would say.

Dabbu's question to people who were good in studies was very simple, "What new have you contributed to the subject?"

Dabbu had contributed most in building 'The Cheap Bastards Diary for Full-time MBA Students'. It laid guidelines for all the 'dos and don'ts' to be followed by them during those two years of rigorous training sessions. This would help them to become an able Manager much ahead of time.

1. Never sit on the last bench; those students are blacklisted, anyway.

2. Never be a front bencher either, nor sit right below the professor's nose. That is a regular '*chaapluss* category' which spoils the professors.

3. If you show that you are giving importance to your professors, you would often find them ignoring you. That's their tendency.

4. Always sit on the middle bench where the potential category sits. MBA Professors have a strange ego, as they are aware that they are building the future *Baniyaas* to run the economy; they always target the student lot that gives them high scope.

5. Never pass all the papers in exams, there have to be some backs; otherwise you would come into the no scope category.

6. They would not invest their efforts in you. Everyone gets placement, it depends upon how you present yourself in the interview. After leaving from college you have to be prepared to face blood suckers with invisible sucking teeth.

7. It is always important to show that you belong to a poor family. Sympathy story does wonders. Always tell that you give tuitions and regularly send money home.

8. Never pay the college fees on time. They anyway charge you a lot. Take that money from parents put it on interest. It will be the first step towards displaying your Management skills.

9. Never waste money in buying books, MBA books are very expensive, and the degree is more about your presence of mind than its retention capacity. Always borrow them from the library or friends.

10. Always make some generous friends who lend their books and notes. But don't forget to make them your partner in crime. There always needs to be a reason, you see.

11. Never sit at home, it's very important to socialize and improve your general knowledge about the rates of new properties coming up. It gives you indications about your future salary meter.

12. Watch a lot of television. Get Boogle alerts on your strong or weak subjects, it gives you reasons to debate with professor and cut the boring lecture short.

13. Always keep one standard power point presentation model; just tailor it as per the case study and keep arguing till the end. There is a lot of scope for debate once you have explored the reason. In Management 2+2 is not expected to be 4, if you have brains you can make it 7 and people will appreciate you for your innovative style of managing that argument and proving your point.

1. Be good at arguments. It shows that your college has invested in the right professors. You might become 'Student of the year.'

2. Never flirt; it's a waste of time. In the corporate world, you will get enough opportunities without any efforts.

This diary had around 101 educative tips and it was fun making it and selling it.

Dabbu was the one to get it printed, and he even managed the sales part of it single-handedly. The book was a simple spiral bound file that was made by using college resources. We earned a lot of money out of it.

We gave that money to 'Scorpio Bank' and for the first time could waive off our loan. That clean status, with no loan, lasted us for only one semester. Our habits had made all of us very dependent on him.'

*****

She smiled again thinking of the book and went back to the paper discussion,

*****

'Our Scorpio Shady, got irritated with Dabbu's fear of exams he said, "Dabbu why can't you think beyond getting papers out, do you even know how we reached those two papers? Who traced that peon? Do you even know how much we suffered?

The worst part is that even after getting the papers, Shark slept. He got through all the papers with good marks, while I could just manage to pass."

"What do you mean by all papers, dude?" screamed Scorpio Shark.

"I mean both the papers, dude," snapped back Shady.

Shark got really pissed "Darling, can you please tell me which papers were they?" The reply was obviously "Accounts and Economics".

"You rascal, do you know they are my graduation subjects, I could have forced you to get other papers in which I desperately needed to pass. Only for friendship's sake, I sacrificed. And I was the one giving you fillers about that peon's schedule. Along with those two liquor bottles, he charged me four grands," said our shark, getting emotional about the money he lost.

Then Bank tried his bit to pacify the agitated minds; "Even I reduced the interest percentage by 0.5% considering the loss."

This added fuel to the already volatile Dabbu; "You say a word and I will kill you Bank. Your darling Gresh created all the problems. We were trying to get those papers sold to university students, and by mistake our agent approached her. This idiot told her mother, who in turn called up the Marketing professor. He could have hanged us all.

Thank god his top floor was empty; he got more worried about reputation of the college than the future of his students. He asked her to calm down by saying, 'Don't worry Mrs Rastogi with this excuse, he might have come to become friends with your daughter. Don't bother about such boys.'

Had the paper got cancelled, it would have been such a big loss Shark, not just money even the hard work would have gone down the drain."

How could Greshma listen, when things were said about her mother? She at once jumped into the conversation without even thinking that there was a fight, just ten minutes back where she was actively involved.

She said to Dabbu, "*Oye* not that I did not apologize mind you. I did and as compensation I sold my mother's gold earrings to give you that money, but mom created such a hue and cry, that I had to get them back the next day. That rascal shopkeeper asked me extra two grands for my own jewellery. I did not have that money so had to take a loan from Neelu. Mom was about to have a heart attack as that piece of jewellery was very close to her heart. It was the first gift; my father had given her before their marriage."

I interrupted, listening to Gresh as even I had to justify my contribution, I said; "Oh yes, how could I forget that one grand which I stole from Papa's pocket to buy new shades of Mac lipstick but had to lend it to Gresh. As far as my lipstick was concerned, I had to borrow money from Bank and that too on full interest. So even I did my share of work."

Gresh got pissed at Bank listening to me, "Except Bank everyone invested. Greedy Bank, how much do you want to earn through us?"

Bank could not take those words and replied as expected, "See Madam it is the basic rule of Management you make money at the expense of other's mistakes and mismanagement. It's as simple as that. You stop making mistakes and start saving money."

There was no point in arguing with Bank, but Gresh had a point, she said, "What if things turned worse at home. My mother could have died had she known the thief. Papa would have not even allowed me to sit for my final exams and married me off."

Bank became a little more emotional; after all, it was Gresh who was in trouble. He said; "I am there for you, Gresh. If they want you to get married, I am ready. You can complete your education and work here, by the time I complete my MS and then we can together stay in the US."

Gresh got irritated and left the place saying, "Oh, just shut up Shashank, and you always find opportunities. How do you manage? I am not accepting your proposal; please stop your efforts on me."

Boys soon lost interest in her drama and got busy in discussing their plan of stealing papers for the last semester. There was no scope for us to fail. We had not been sharing results at home for all the obvious and non-obvious reasons.

Master Mind was master of plans. The major contributors to this skill were daily breakfast sessions with his father, who always had brain teasers for him. Mr Kishore Keval Rajput made sure that his son had a sharp sense of business, and his mind was always put agile. 'Paper stealing plan' was peanuts for Master Mind.

Dabbu said, "Master Mind which plan are we going to follow this time plan 1, 2 or 3. I want to clear all the papers in this attempt anyhow; I have already booked my tickets for Leh-Ladakh. It was not easy to convince 'the Don', my father, for this trip. I can't miss it. If I fail, papa will make me assist some shopkeeper and two years down the line, he will sell me to some rich girl's father."

Everyone laughed at his statement but Keval was very sure. He said; "No plans this time, its only action, all you guys need to do is, just follow the instructions. Meet me close to Mathew's office tomorrow morning at 10:30 sharp."

Mathew Sir was our college Director and everyone was scared of him. He had decided to take our college to being No.1 in Madhya Pradesh. With his tireless efforts our college had become autonomous that year. Of course, he did use the influence of Master Mind's father. In just five years' time, it had become student's first choice of the locals, for Management course.

"Ok done," said Dabbu on behalf of all of us.

All reached on time the next day, "Hi guys," said Master.

Shark got a little annoyed with him, "What were you doing with Mathew's peon? Everyone knows us and our objectives. Mathew is just looking for an opportunity to get us hooked, and he is well aware of what we did last year. You are giving direct invitation to a serious problem, Master."

The confident man said, "Guys, you don't have to worry about that; and Shark, I only want you to follow and leave the rest to me. Exam papers are set just seven days before the date and go for printing just three days before. The best part is that this time, papers are made by Mathew Sir and will be saved in his computer. He will be taking the print himself, but his folder has no access. So, during the afternoon when he goes to the canteen for lunch this peon would give us access to his room, Dabbu will quickly get the folder in my pen drive and we will share three questions of each paper amongst us."

Dabbu got pissed listening to him; he did not understand the logic of three questions; "Why only three?"

Master had always been smart; "Darling, that is only because out of the seven options three are enough to pass. Have you ever written answers to more than three? Moreover, this time the papers are not going to the university and so we will not be able to use our usual strategy of paying money to the clerks to change the marks. Now Mathew Sir would not tolerate any nonsense. And if I will give all seven questions, trust me, we would all choose same three to answer due to the similar manufacturing defect that we are born with."

Dabbu was relaxed on listening to the explanation; "Am fine with it. I only need to pass. As long as there are three questions of all the twelve subjects that I am supposed to pass, I can take any risk in the world." Dabbu was very daring but would not move a single step ahead unless he was convinced with the idea.

We were scared of Dabbu's rigidness at times. Shashank once informed him about a junior who stayed next to his house had spoken wrong about his family; the next day that junior was in hospital. We used to be very cautious about what we said to him.

Chapter 5

The Pledge to be Together

In the darkest of the days I swear

As promised, I will always be there

It isn't your beautiful eyes or lovely long hair

It's your pure heart that binds me to you for all I care

Neelakshi enjoyed the joy ride of her old days.

*****

'Once the exams were over, it was only placement in mind. We had not appeared for any of the interviews organized by the college. Jitters before the interview, and the stress of performance never excited us.

Basically, it was the fear of being rejected that always held us back, and moreover our poor grades forced us to wear a pretence.

After the last paper, our 'Scorpio Bank', out of all the people came running to us, flaunting the question sheet. He practically had nothing to do in India once he was set to go for his MS, to the US. I knew he was teasing us, "Guys have you all completed your project? Our viva is on 30th and based on that performance we would be eligible for the final round of campus interview."

"Are you mad who would allow us to sit for the placements?" said Shady getting irritated with him. It was Master then, who took over, as he could sense our anxiety, "*Bhai* Shady do you even know what you want to do in life?"

"Master, I know what I don't want to do and I am very clear about that," he replied.

Somewhere deep inside, we all knew that we were not clear about what we exactly wanted. We knew that we were all running away from our inner fears. These fears were real and well-defined yet complicated enough to express. We had a faint glimpse of what we wanted, but painting the real picture needs courage. We were scared to bring the actual image of our dreams to light. Probably the best option for us was to run away from what we could not do.

Tension was at its peak and Shady wanted a cigarette. Master got irritated at this and he threw a pack at him saying, "*Ye le salee aur tera MP ka dimag lagana band kar abhi.* We will definitely need it for our next plan."

"One more plan?" said Gresh, spreading her hands across the table, almost dropping the Tepsi bottle. Thankfully Bank saved it. It was still half-filled. And that too was taken on loan.

Our college was one of the rare places which had both Tepsi and Soke. Despite of Soco Cola's branding, shouting loud enough to declare about the investments done in the canteen, Kallu Bhaiya happily served Tepsi when ordered. We used to have a group account in the canteen that was settled only when college re-opened after the semester break.

Our favourite Kallu Bhaiya used to make yummy *Samosas*. Our canteen was very spacious and most of our strategies were made there. It was a nice and calm place unlike other college canteens. Sometimes we could even listen to music after 3:00 pm. Since it was close to the dam, the place had its own charm and had lot of visitors, after college hours.

Passing in the exams was guaranteed, but placement was beyond imagination, so 'what next' was a big question for us. As usual, we all surrendered to Master Mind's plans.

Gresh's astrologer had thankfully given her a grace period of two more years. Planet Mars; was still in the most inappropriate house of her horoscope. This came as a blessing in disguise for her, but for me, things were still difficult.

My time of freedom was over. Papa had already arranged a meeting with Singh uncle's son, much before my results could hit his ears. Not that my father was a broad-minded person to allow a meeting before marriage, but since the guy stayed in the US and had his own views about marriage, papa was left with no choice but to agree.

Gresh declared in the canteen that she would accept Shashank's proposal only on the condition that he would become independent in two years' time and meet her parents. In the meanwhile, she would build her career. Shashank agreed at once.

I used to wonder why everything was so simple for her, but equally difficult for me. It was me who wanted to have a career and a non-Rajput boyfriend, but everything right was happening to her. That moment I felt too jealous of her and equally insecure of my own life.

Her mother would never send her out alone, because she feared someone would take advantage of her little doll. I was seeing that doll, grown bold enough to declare her life's biggest decision in front of everyone, irrespective of her mother's fear.

She looked so fearless to me, almost like a source of inspiration. I kept on looking at her till Kallu Bhaiya came to our table.

He got very emotional since it was officially supposed to be our last day in the college, "*Bolo Master Bhaiya... tum log to bahut pad likh gaye ho... ab to chale jaoge hamesha ke liye.*"

Master was also touched, with a smile he reciprocated; "*Kyun bolte ho aaise bhaiya... ek kadak chai sab ke liye... tumhare thumke ke saath aur raam bhai ke gussee aur gali ke saath laao... bill to humne abi tak chukaya nahi hai... 3000 rupiya ho gaya hai pichale teen maheene se. Baad mein de denge.*"Kallu Bhaiya was just an employee of Rambhai canteen but was very generous to us. "*Aree Bhaiya abhi leyoo chai aur samose bhi... Uss Ram Bhai Ki to aaisi ki taisi. Tumko paise jab dena ho tab dena. Nahi ho to matt dena. Par yahaan aate rehena jaroor.*"

His *Samosas* were world famous, even the heroine of our college, whom we called "Miss Show off" got her *US wali Pammi aunty* to taste them. Her aunty liked them too and at once went into the kitchen to know the recipe. It was a different story though, that she did not even know the difference between '*jeera* and *raai*', yet she wanted to try her hands at making them.

As Kallu Bhaiya left I started looking at Gresh again, she was looking at Shashank as if she was in love with him. Somewhere I knew it was not love, he was just a standby option, till she lived her dreams.

As I was lost Master had already started sharing his Plan1, according to which it was only boys who were supposed to be a part of the next adventure. He had his own sweet reasons for that.

He started addressing without any intimation, "Bank is all set to go to the US, Gresh will be taking up some teaching job here, since HR is not a field which would fetch her a good job easily, I am going to get into business, Dabbu it would be great if you explore more on travel and tourism and then you can start your own business, Shady and Shark should be going out of Bhopal, to explore better opportunities and my darling Charas after we are 35 years old I will be there for you. So till then you can do whatever you want –work, enjoy, get married, have kids with any guy of your choice and when you are fed up with that routine life you can leave all of them and come to me, I will treat you like my queen."

That was an insult to me, and I felt like killing him that day itself. He tried to put me down in front of everyone. It was for the first time I realized the difference between a friend and a guy who is supposed to be a best friend. I left the place and went to the other table in anger. The innocent side of me wanted to be a part of the adventure, ignoring all the odds. Nothing was in my favour, but what pinched me the most was being written off like this. Scorpio trait, I guess.

Looking at this, Gresh came to my table and tried to pacify; "*Dil par matt le yaar*...you know him, right? Just come."

"What do you mean, Gresh?" I snapped back at her.

"That is his style of proposing to you. Why are you taking it so negatively?" she said, and I agreed to go back to the table, not because I had forgiven Keval but because I needed a strong reason to forgive him.

We were friends since childhood, yet Keval dared to speak with me that way, and even Gresh had been selfish to me.'

*****

It was difficult for Neelakshi to accept that both her childhood friends had taken her presence in their life too much for granted. It was just that she had always ignored many things. She lay quiet for a little while and then went back to the memories of her old days.

*****

'After the fight we all zeroed in on plan 2, that included girls and the next action was to meet Ballu Bhaiya. A really funny guy, who had all connections in the world, probably he was also associated with the underworld. He was a champ at getting any and every kind of work done. He was a much-modified version of our Scorpio Shark.

Not just that, he also was an astrologer. He could make prediction through vibes, by just looking at the person.

He was a short guy, with his skin as thin as paper, he had a low pitch voice that could be confused with that of an old woman. My job was to do a follow up with him till he confirmed a meeting time. Getting an appointment from him was the most difficult task in the world. He definitely required a Secretary but preferred to handle everything by himself.

He believed that middlemen spoil the work, when in his thirty-five years of career he did not need anybody, why would he need now. All the people who approached him were important to him. He seemed to be more occupied than even the Prime Minister of our country.

So finally, with all my hard work, we got an appointment with him at his place. It was a 30 minutes time slot, not a minute more or a minute less. He was an interesting guy. His stories made us roll over the entire place with laughter. However, there was a subtle message for us in the under stated tones.'

*****

Neelakshi thought of the amusing expression on Dabbu's face after they listened to Pavan Mishra story.

*****

He said, "Ballu Bhaiya, how is it possible? You mean Pavan Mishra used his wife's London University MBA degree as his own. Prepared fake experience certificate of some IT company, gave his wife's number as his ex-Boss for reference check and secured a job in the US."

"Yes Karan, not just that he also bought a house and paid back the loan that his father had taken for his education. Today he is happily settled in the US. I just showed him a way and he walked the entire road all by himself," replied Ballu Bhaiya.

For Ballu Bhaiya, such things were just like a cakewalk. He continued to say as we looked at him with our eyes wide open and jaws dropped down, "The amount of brain that our country has is unbeatable. You just need to know how to use it. A little courage and these hurdles automatically become small. Small things should never affect your big dreams," he said and then smiled, indicating that twenty minutes were over.

He still concluded his speech with a statement, "*Main Janata Ka Sevak hun Desh Ki unnati Chahata hun.*"

What a '*Janata Ka Sevak*' he was. Our problem was absolutely nothing for him. He called up someone, just to mention that he had some youngsters who fall in stage 4.75

The phrase - stage 4.75 was even more amusing to know, as we got into the details.

They worked out a plan for us. According to them every problem fell in some category and demanded specific resources. This super-efficient Ballu Bhaiya's team could challenge the best of the business consultancies in the world.

If these consultancies used Harvard graduates to make policies and systems for the virtual world, Ballu Bhaiya's tenth fail employees knew how to break those systems and crash them down to ash.

It's all about how you execute your brain's efficiency. Everything around is crystal clear, if your brain has the capacity to scan through. Even Dabbu was very impressed. He was the only one to have kept in touch with Ballu Bhaiya till date.

The outcome of the meeting was to work towards a good corporate exposure. This demanded us to move to a bigger city. They showed us a slide in which they spoke about common problems faced by small town youngsters like us.

1. Communication - We were big time *sheikh chillis* our *batoolebaazi* had no end but for clearing interviews there is no scope for such skills. Our performance was required to be more artistic, blended well with a tint of professionalism.

2. Resume–It needs to look inviting, rich and intelligent. A little work experience would add on.

3. Mark Sheet–Required to be polished.

4. College–A good name works. He suggested that we get enrolled into a one-year distant learning course from IIIM.

    Such courses add value to the resume, whether you get the degree or not.

5. Package–Since we decided to show work experience. A salary slip with decent package was a must. He wanted us to show that the company from where we did our summer training, absorbed us as Management Trainees. That was the safest bet.

6.   References–Preparing a good reference back up for us, was not a problem for him.

Ballu Bhaiya believed in the philosophy of going against the crowd; for him it was an art. It's a journey, and you lose nothing. Our experience all through, only adds value to the quality of life we live. After all, there is a blind turn pre-decided, where one meets death. So why walk the straight road, instead explore new roads to make life worth living.

We felt as if his philosophy of life was blending with ours, but we still had a long way to go.

Since all corporate houses had their branch offices in Bhopal, Ballu Bhaiya arranged a one-week workshop for all four of us. It helped us understand the Standard Operating Procedures of our chosen companies.

Meanwhile, based on our basic information, Ballu Bhaiya prepared all the necessary documents. He suggested that we make PAN card and keep our basic salary as 5000/- per month.

We realized for the first time that wrong things were equally simple and can be done by staying within the system. There is no need to complicate the process and go against the guidelines.

There is nothing like pure Black or pure White in the system, everything is grey and the efficiency of human mind and execution skill lies in achieving the most proximate shade of either extreme and yet proving it to be pure white.

Ballu Bhaiya was our saviour. He usually charged heavy for his tips on astrology, to avoid such discussions, but on the last day when we went to collect our documents, he said, "Just remember one thing kids, land will bind you and your friendship together and money will set you all apart."

We did not understand the depth of those words back then, but whatever we understood of it was good enough to keep us together.

We decided to dine out that night and thus informed our parents about the same. We walked down to our favourite eating joint in Bitthan Market, close to *Ballu Bhaiya's* place.

Everyone was making fun of me there, as they knew convincing my father was the biggest task in hand.

In that *masti* Keval suddenly turned poetic and said a few words in my praise, which were hard to believe –

"Teri hanseen mein chupi hai ek adaa kaatil

chaloo kareen teri akhoon se batein

aur sajayeen aaj sitaaroon sang jashnee mehefil."

"What is this Master?" I blushed and turned almost red; I did not know where to look.

"Nothing *Charas*, for the first time I noticed something more about you," he said and started laughing like a crook. I did not respond.

That night was very strange, everything was getting too serious, and we were just not prepared for anything. *Mazaak mazaak mein,* we had actually taken a very bold decision.

We had decided to move to another city, to a Metro, "How will I convince my father?" I thought.

Meanwhile, I had my official date with Singh uncle's son. He clarified that he was in live-in relation with a French girl in the US, and would marry only her. He expected me to say 'no' to the proposal and not disclose his love story to anyone. But I did not agree with him and said exactly what he had said to me. Papa went mad at uncle. He allowed our meeting only because he was sure it would materialize into marriage.

Taking advantage of the situation, Gresh and I tried talking to Papa about going to Pune. Unfortunately, it all boomeranged on us and I could not go out of the house till my results were out. Thankfully I passed with good numbers, but to convince Papa was still a tough task.

Time had now come to take the decision, instead of waiting for permission. I declared that I am going to Pune with Gresh. There were no dialogues between Papa and me for a very long time, till finally he agreed.

It was always a mystery for me; I could never believe how it is so easy for a father to trust a strange man for his daughter, but so difficult to trust his own daughter's ability to take charge of her life. It's always the mind which rules when it is between two men, but it's the confused mind which surrenders otherwise. And men don't like to give up, hence for a girl's father the game continues with the other man of his choice.

*****

Neelakshi smiled to herself thinking of the tough fight she gave to her father and then started crying, thinking of the man she chose against her father. It was complicated, but that is how she wanted it. Both men were dead. Where once she was the victory trophy of the game, today she stood alone on the play field with no one to compete for.

She controlled herself, trying not to get carried away, and went back to the old days, where everything was set for them to leave for Pune.

*****

'By now our training was over and we had all the required documents. We learnt three basic rules about the corporate world from our one-week corporate training. They became our "*Success Mantras*" -

1. Always be prepared to cover your senior's mistakes and make sure he is informed you have done it, of course in the politest way possible.

2. Never let your juniors make any mistake that would get you into trouble.

3. Always be alert and ready to find mistakes in people at your level, they should never be able to prove themselves better than you.

The tickets were booked for a month later, as we needed some time to shop, prepare everyone to be emotionally strong, and collect money from all the possible sources. It needed to be enough for at least three months.

Ballu Bhaiya's file had a database of job consultants in Pune and Mumbai. We floated our resume to them fifteen days before we left. All the friends and seniors were contacted, and the network was well set. As per 'Plan 4' all the seven of us went to Pune to see what destiny had in store for us. Three of them joined for a little time till the remaining four settled there.'

*****

Chapter 6

The New World

I can't define in just a few words

Beauty of the new place with chirping birds

Some people here behave like nerds

There is always a black sheep in the herds

Neelakshi thought about the time when they were leaving for Pune,

*****

The D-day had come; 11th June 2003 and 11:20pm was our train to Pune–the Jhelum Express.

Our parents were very nervous; they had come to drop us at Habibganj Station. I still remember my father's face; he hated going to see off anyone. The only time he loved coming to the station was to receive someone.

As the train was coming closer, Papa tried to control his emotions. It was me who was going, *'his jigar ka tukda'*. He was not really sure of how to react. Though I was going with Gresh, there were guys along.

I had not told him about the guys. He would have got me married that day itself. It was clear from his eyes that he felt betrayed.

*****

Neelakshi visualized the way train had stopped with a jerk, making everything still for her. The jerk was strong enough to get her out of her thoughts, as she saw mobile phone ringing. The call was from her office.

She saw the time, it was only 3:15 pm and Little Kishore was fast asleep. She could see the tiredness on his face.

Little Kishore was born on the day Neelakshi's father passed away. He did not see his grandson. Neelakshi had no regrets. The set of rules laid by her father and the society would have never given her what she had. If being alone was destiny, then she was prepared for it. She always saw her mother and grandmother unhappy with their life. They used to grumble within the four walls and had no one to hear; they were married, had children, yet were always alone.

Neelakshi rejected the call and sent a message to her secretary, 'busy will call back'.

"Madam something serious," the mobile phone beeped. Neelakshi called back.

"Good evening, Madam," said a quirky voice from the other side.

"Yes, Rosa, what is it?"

"Madam, there were two men in office who came without any prior appointment, just before lunch and directly went to General Manager Finance's cabin," the voice replied.

"So?"

"I don't know how to explain Madam, but they did not seem to be the GM's friends."

"What are you trying to say, Rosa? Am I supposed to keep a track of who comes to meet Mr Chattarjee for lunch?"

"Ok, let me try Madam. We have doubts it was policemen without uniform and they have instructed Mr Chattarjee not to disclose about their visit to you."

"What?"

"Yes Madam, office boy got the hint of it, he ran to inform me, and I called you immediately. I guess you could see them on your CCTV unless Mr Chattarjee deletes the footage. I don't know if it was in the context of the Body wash campaign."

"Don't worry Rosa, you take-care and don't disclose it to anyone."

Neelakshi disconnected the phone. She got the hint that police had started its investigation against Keval's death, suspecting it to be a murder. There were no clues found as such that would confirm a murder though.

She did not want to disturb her mind with the present and so escaped back to where the train had stopped with a jerk,

*****

'Papa went emotional just with the thought, that the door of compartment would open and close, creating miles distance between us. The train would take his daughter in, and send her away from him.

It was just a two-minute stop and enough for him to create a drama; after all, he was my father. Just before the train could stop, he said to all of us, "kid's time has finally come, I wish you all success. Just remember, these two girls are your responsibility and if anything happens to them, I will not spare you." I didn't know where to hide my face.

Gresh's dadi had expired so no one from her family could come. They had all gone to their native village, and that was the main reason my father had come. I still regret that.

Dabbu's *chaachi* got offended and she asked Papa to take me back home at once. She had arranged for our stay in her friend's place, but those words from Papa had hurt her a lot.

That drama took one full minute to complete. *Papa ki purii izzat station par hi utaar di thi aunty ne.* That was the second time my father felt bad because of me. But I had to go, and there could be no stopping me.

By then everyone was in and I was the only one trying to figure out what was happening. Train was just about to move and suddenly Papa asked me to get into the train. For once, I thought he cared for me and my dreams.

As soon as I threw my luggage inside, the train moved and I was rushed into the moving train. Soon I realized it was not care for me but care for his *'Rajput Shaan'* in front of Dabbu's *chaachi*, which compelled him to give me the permission. I could have died in this adventure.'

*****

Neelakshi took a little break from her old days and looked at her phone again. There was a message from Greshma, "tried calling you, I am on my way to Pahargarh".

She did not respond to the message as somewhere Neelakshi was not very comfortable with Greshma's probing attitude. As a journalist, she had a habit of giving her opinion while Neelakshi was not in a state of mind to accept anybody's opinion. She had done what she felt right and wanted to stay with it without giving any justification. She did not want to answer any of Greshma's questions.

Neelakshi just tried to get out of the present and dive back into the pool of her old days,

*****

'Getting inside a moving train was a sick idea, and my father agreed to get me in. I will never be able to understand these Rajput men. Its only blood and women that obsess them; when it comes to common sense, they seem to have nothing at all. It was already 11:25 pm, and I was dead tired.

"Happy with your DDLJ adventure?" said Gresh, which irritated me even more. I did not respond to her and went off to sleep in my allotted seat that was just below hers. Next day morning for all of us was at 01:30 in the afternoon, with people shouting '*Anda sandwich, vada paav, bhaji paav, poori bhajhi*', at Manmaar Station.

None of us had brushed our teeth; it wasn't difficult to imagine the condition of the washroom by then, dirty and without water. We did not have the courage to check it ourself, nor had the luxury to waste so much of Mineral water. I was dying to use that bottle. Shark gave me such a dirty look, as if I was stealing something that I withdrew. The most sensible option for us was to eat quietly without even discussing about it.

Shady found it very fascinating, for him looking Ms Perfect in such a messed-up state was next to impossible. He tried hard to capture me in his mobile camera, but thankfully his battery did not support. He still did not give up and said a few lines in my praise that were equally irritating -

Wo salaa chai mein dubo kar,

Biscuit ki tarah make up nigal gaya

aur mera Ms Perfect look

jo dhoop mein chamakte barf ke mahal sa tha

chaand ki garmi se hi pighal gaya

I did not respond to him either. Somewhere I started getting a feeling that everyone had teamed up against me, though they weren't harsh, somewhere something was hurting me.

We reached station at 4:30pm. It wasn't a very happening place. Dabbu's cousin brother came to receive us with a bunch of his hostel friends. To take six people and twelve luggage bags to some place called *Nal Stop* in Pune, *rickshawala* charged us Rs.200/- per rickshaw. And we took around 4 rickshaws.

Rs.800/-went off our pocket the very first day. It was a big amount for jobless people like us. First, we went to our new place, where Dabbu's *chaachi*'s friend, our PG aunty, Mrs Datee welcomed all of us. She seemed to be a good lady. Complementing the surname, her teeth looked very prominent on her face. She was very fair, very thin, had blue eyes and lovely curly hair. Though she was short, her tongue was long enough to cover her height.

Both me and Gresh had a quick bath in turns and rushed to see the guys flat that was in the next building. It was awesome with huge windows, and two big balconies. We had hardly seen flats in our city, so for us climbing steps to enter a house was an amazing experience.

We were hungry and wanted to eat, but since Aunty had invited us for dinner, we did not eat anything. Shark had fixed interviews with placement agencies from Tuesday onwards. So, we had two days to adjust in the new environment.

Dinner time at Auntie's place was the best experience. Her food was really yum and we were happy that we would get good home-made food.

Aunty assured that everything would be fine and we would never have any problem in looking for job. Her daughter and son-in-law, who were working in a call centre, had good contacts.

As she served us sweet dish, which was supposedly the last round of our meal, her sweet talks became even more aggressive. She said, "*Beta* I am like your mother. Never feel alone in this city. When you come home tired from office, you can always get home made food, I will make it for you. In fact, you need not pay me every day, you can pay me in advance 75x2 times meal in a day x 30 days a month exactly – 4500/- per head so that I could buy all the stuff in advance and cook whatever you want.

I will not charge you for morning tea. But yes, if you want milk then it will be extra 600/- so in just 5100 you will be through with your lunch, dinner and morning milk tension. I guess with milk you will keep some biscuits and snacks also. I can bring them for you all, so with only Rs.5600/- your food problem will get solved. And I am not even asking you to pay for the utensils or the maid, helper, gas, etc. It will be all free of cost. I will bear that cost myself for you. After all you are like my own kids. In hotels you don't get a *thaali* for less than Rs.150/- and that too not as tasty as home-made food."

That was too generous of Aunty. We could never forget her help; at the time we needed the most.

We had no words to say; almost dumb struck, we just stood there looking at her lips move. Master then took over.

He said, "Oh Aunty, that is so nice of you, thank you so much for the offer, but we have got two months grocery with us, as we were not expecting such a generosity from you. Our flat also has gas and other facilities.

Whenever we feel like eating, we will drop into your house and once our stuff is about to get over, we will inform you in advance so that you have enough time. It's really nice of you to be so considerate."

The lady would have otherwise made us paupers for her economic growth. Master knew we needed a break from her. He said, "Aunty, there is some stuff we need to give to these girls; we will drop them back before the deadline. Is there anything you want us to pay now?"

The lady understood her sweet talks had failed, so she cunningly replied; "*No, no beta* don't worry, I will adjust today's food money from the deposit of these girls since you are not having food from me every day. I am your Aunty; never feel shy of sharing any problem with me."

"Thank you, aunty, we will be back in an hour," I replied and we hurried down for some fresh air.

She was greedy; she did not stop, I could still hear her say; "Sure *beta,* just make a note. If you are late from the given deadline, then you would have to pay a penalty. I will discuss that with you when you return back or may be tomorrow morning; I guess you girls must be tired today."

Oh god I just thought I would kill her in the next one week; yet very politely replied back; "*Ji Aunty*. See you by 10:30."

As we went down the steps our shoes made loud noise, and we rushed as if the prisoners were given a chance to escape.'

*****

The word 'prisoner' struck Neelakshi, and she suddenly froze, as she imagined herself standing behind the bars and policemen doing their investigation with her. The newspaper headline flashed in her mind again and again. She could not take it further and tried to sleep, but was disturbed by the knock on her room's door.

She wanted to shout aloud, but resisted. She covered Little Kishore properly with the blanket, lowered temperature of AC, and opened the huge wooden door.

It was Ramu Kaka again; he stood with his eyes lowered straight at 90 degree to the ground. She looked at the wall clock; it was 5:40 pm.

"*Hukum, Greshamji aapse milne aai hain. Maa Sahab ne unko badi baithak mein bhaithaaya hai aur aapse milaane ke liye bola hai.*"

"Oh Gresh," Neelakshi said to herself and continued to say the rest in her mind; "I need you so badly. But have you come to scratch my wounds? I will not tell you anything, Gresh."

She hurried to the *Badi Baithak* and asked Ramu Kaka to keep Greshma's luggage in the next room.

For Neelakshi, it was as if Greshma just walked out from the pages of time and was standing right in front of her. Her eyes still had the same spark. They both hugged and wept for some time, consoling each other, and trying to come to terms with the reality. Neelakshi took Greshma to the guest room. They were both quiet for a very long time until Greshma took out a hundred rupee note from her purse, "Neelu do you remember this?"

"Gresh this looks like the same hundred rupees note which we took out from the ATM after my first salary. And I gave it to you." Neelakshi took that note and kept on looking at it like a child.

"I am always there with you Neelu."

"I know Gresh, I know it very well," said Neelakshi in agreement.

Greshma's big round eyes became very tiny, yet were shining with the same spark. Her face turned red as tears rolled down her cheeks.

"Before coming here, I spoke to Dabbu, and he says things are getting on a very complicated track. We might come on roads."

"He is mad Gresh and you too are mad. Please stop your nonsensical subject and relax for some time. Stop listening to Dabbu, for God's sake. Does he even have a brain of his own? Why do you have a soft corner for him? Is Shashank not keeping you happy?"

"Shut up, Neelu. Mind your words."

The whole conversation turned into a tension until Ramu Kaka came with coffee and something to eat. Neelakshi tried to cease the fire by diverting the conversation to old days.

"Gresh, do you remember our first meeting with Datee Aunty?"

Greshma too tried her best to get back and warmly reciprocated. "She was crazy, dude. Introduction *hua nahi ke usne meter chalu kar diya*. Every time she used to give *hool* of cutting the deposit money. First day itself she swiped Rs.1350/- from that money. I still remember that number. Shashank did the entire calculation as Aunty spoke."

"Bank had been really handy at times. Do you remember how he made us understand these small calculations so that no one could fool us?"

"Yes, Neelu, I do remember," she said with tiredness in her voice.

Neelakshi made her comfortable and soon Greshma slept. It was only 6:00 pm now. Maa Sahab never liked anyone sleeping in the evening. According to her, it brought negative energy in the house. But today she herself was with no energy.

Neelakshi went back to her room. She wanted those good memories to accompany her; it was as if they had possessed her.

It was only in those days where she could now find her Man. He was so perfect for her.

*****

'It was raining heavily. All wet, we hurried back and rang the bell. It was sharp 9:55, and we were home well before time. Aunty let us in, greeted us with a smile and gave a set of keys and a list of rules and regulations which, if not followed, would lead us to penalty.

Her main objective was to eat away all our deposit money and we had decided that we will not let her do that.

The craziest thing was that Aunty said she would be staying at her daughter's place, and if there was any problem, we could call on her mobile. She left us alone in the house without even giving her mobile number.

That was the scariest part of the whole episode.'

*****

Life for Neelakshi had always been adventurous. It is true that you have a story to tell only if you have travelled. She had travelled alone a long way, yet there was a lot more to explore. Keval was no more there to walk with her, but she knew her journey would not stop. She went back to thinking of the part of life where Greshma had walked with her.

*****

On seeing Aunty go, Gresh went furious and started yelling, "Is this woman mad? We came into this house only because we thought, she would stay with us. Our boys are anyways not allowed in the house. I heard from someone that PG system in Pune is scary; they hide cameras in the room."

"Gresh just shut up and please sleep tonight, tomorrow we will see what is to be done."

But that was not enough to calm her down; she just went on with her funny list of doubts – "Neelu I have my doubts, I think Aunty has put something in our food. I am feeling a bit drowsy. Please check if the room doors are locked. I hope there is no secret door which Aunty left open for a rapist to enter. Even this balcony is open. How long does it take for a person to break the door, anyone can walk in."?

"Of all the people in the world Gresh, why would a rapist come? Talk sense for God's sake."

"You never believe me Neelu; now see for yourself when he comes."

We made sure we double locked our room door, switched off the lights and slept, until at 3:00 in the night when Gresh woke me up with a loud scream. That was the weirdest scream I ever heard from her. I did not have the courage to open my eyes and see someone over Gresh.

I regretted not paying heed to her words, in despair I tried to reach the switch board.

It took a while for the light to turn on, meanwhile I was wondering if she was wearing anything or had the rapist taken everything off her.

Gresh managed to see me "Oh God Neelu it's you, thank God, I thought there was a rapist. We will just keep the lights on and sleep tonight, please." I felt like killing her, but we finally slept without another word. The next morning for us started with a mad doorbell at 5:30 am. We woke up to find it was the *newspaperwala*. Aunty had asked him to check if we needed newspapers.

We checked for the hidden cameras, but could not find any, so concluded that Aunty wanted us to settle the first night and then she would put the camera in our absence. Gresh believed that she will send the rapist in any of the coming nights.

We decided to put a new lock in our room and not give her the keys, even if she pestered us for it.

The second door bell was just ten minutes later, and it was too irritating, Gresh went to the door and saw Shark and Master, who was not in his formals, it was clear that there was something wrong but we did not make any guess.

Strangely, they thought that something happened to us last night. There was news on the national television channel, just a few minutes before, which flashed about some police raid in Zelam Apartment, our building at 3:00 in the morning. That was exactly when Gresh had screamed.

Boys were relieved to see us alive; Shark's imagination led him to think that we were murdered. Master insisted on us calling our fathers and informing them that we were fine.

Quickly we brushed our teeth and went down. As we were going down, Shark pointed out at a flat, "That is the place, just look at the size of the lock. People carried out some illegal transactions from there."

We went straight to the grocery shop, which was just a few steps away from the boys building. Guys had already made a to-do list and grocery list along with the budget.

Cooking was our part but, effect of the pathetic '*Khichdi*' that I made was so powerful that everyone got back to work immediately. It was decided that we will make a collective budget; this would bring us all to one level. Nobody wanted a call centre job, so that option was ruled out.

Total we had around one lakh rupees, which were more than enough for three months sustenance. Now we were no longer worried about money, we were "a one lakh Scorpio Group". Shady and Bank had worked on the budget allocation and we opted for mess food.

For initial ten days we all did not do anything that Master said but none of us got job either, so finally we agreed to his plan and to our surprise we started getting offer letters in just one week's time.

Gresh took job as a Regional Marketing Executive in a newspaper, with an initial package of ten grand per month along with a mobile phone and petrol allowance.

I got into a placement agency as Junior Recruitment Executive with just one-month training and then confirmation based on performance.

Shady got into operations with a very big automobile company, he was sick of the sales job offers. Even if he applied for some other position, they would direct him to their sales head. In the end, he fought with the HR manager of this company and got into the profile of his interest.

Shark was full on *Jugadu*; he already had some connections that helped him to get a job in a Bank. There was a big fight between Master Mind and Shark when he declared about his job. Master wanted him to join some Non-Profit Organization, but Shark had his own reservations. He wanted quick money.

Master Mind was happy with everybody else's placement; it seemed that there was some objective behind whatever we were doing.

Soon all the strugglers started going to office. We shifted to a girl's apartment just below the boys' apartment. We had a *Mausi* to cook for us. We had plenty of money now for survival. All chose the Date of Joining as 1st of July so that we could have enough fun with our supporters till then. I wanted to spend more time with Keval. Now it was no more than an attention-grabbing urge, it had moved on to something more.

Keval would drop me to office every morning and every evening would wait for one hour in front of my office to pick me up. I used to eagerly wait for the office to get over. There was something that was driving me close to him, he reciprocated but in a strange way.

Shady had to get rid of his ponytail, because his boss did not like it for obvious reasons. After coming home, we used to love sharing the happenings of the whole day, but I would keep mum about my time after office and before reaching home. That was special and was only for me. Dinner was made in the boys' flat. We used to go up, to eat and be there till late night until we were dead tired.

In the two months' time the interior of boys' flat had changed. It had a big hall, with a lovely coffee shop type look so that we could enjoy our time there. Master Mind had got all this done for us.

Even when we joined office, the other three musketeers decided to be there till we actually settled.

Dabbu visited a lot of places in Maharashtra to understand the tourism business there.

Bank would always be busy on his laptop and with his documents, as he decided to board from Mumbai International Airport instead of Delhi. Visa, loan and other formalities were done by him in this free time.

Master Mind was Master of his own games, only God knew what he was up to. But yes, he would always be on time when it came to dropping me or picking me up from office.

In all the three months he kept his first Saturday of the month commitment as it was. It was strange as always, he hardly spoke to his father during that time,' thought Neelakshi and closed her eyes to take a little break from those days.

*****

"Gresh" Neelakshi thought and rushed to her room to wake her up, but she was already awake, sitting with Maa Sahab and chatting.

Maa Sahab was an extremely strong woman and she would never let anyone get the hint of what she would think. For one second Neelakshi thought that those were the same traits that Keval possessed, and the very next second she dismissed the thought and went inside the room.

"*Maa Sahab Pranaam,*" said Neelakshi.

"*Khush raho Bahoo.*"

"*Maa Sahab ye kya...*" Neelakshi looked at Maa Sahab with tears in her eyes.

"I never understood the equation between you and Keval, but I believe in what I see. I saw you as the only woman in my son's life to the extent that you agreed to become the mother of his child. I always believe in rituals, but this generation is far away from understanding them. I don't blame you, but if I have the authority, this is how I want you to be," said Maa Sahab.

She changed Neelakshi's life with just a few 'I' coupled with some words.

"What else do I want, Maa Sahab?" said Neelakshi and Maa Sahab left, carrying an expression of satisfaction on her face.

Both mother-in-law and daughter-in-law were happy with their newly discovered relation, but Greshma was absolutely against it.

Greshma's inner voice spoke to her in irritation, "How can Neel spoil her complete life for a man who is no more?"

So, what if little Kishore is her son, she could have more children if she marries a better man. After all, who knows this truth? But why is she succumbing to this woman? Why did she even succumb to Keval?"

She banged her fist to the wall behind the sofa and hurt herself, but still kept thinking, "Why are these mother and son so intimidating? Even I succumbed to Master once," she remembered the darkest night of her life and shook her head to knock the thought off. He did not have honest eyes, which she wanted. Greshma was lost in herself till her mobile phone ringtone got her back.

Everybody's attention was diverted to the mobile phone ring; it was an old song sung by Late Kishore Kumar and it did succeed in changing moods of people in the room.

She looked at the phone and said, "Oh its Shark calling."

"Hi Gresh, are you with Neelu?"

"Yes. Why?"

"Just wanted to inform that I am coming tomorrow morning," said Raj Bhandari, who was now the Director at Association of Indian Corporate (AIC), the most profitable, Non-Profit Organization. It grew to that level under his expert guidance.

He sung his song to the glory, and his lies added flavour to the achievements he had to his credit. Greshma remembered interviewing him on many occasions for her television shows. He gave stories that got the show huge TRPs. So, for her, he was the man whom she could never disappoint.

*****

Greshma remained silent for some time and then turned to Neelakshi; "Neelu when I can, why can't you move on?"

Neelakshi spoke after a long gap, but her conversation was from a very different angle as if to say please don't interfere in my personal life.

"Gresh do you remember once, when we got frustrated during our initial job hunt days, in Pune Master once joked on us. He said that we will open a Drama company if nothing works out for us.

He would design the drama, Shark would sing, you would be the master of the ceremony, I would dance and act to his lines, Bank would get the financers, Dabbu would sell the tickets and Shady would add spice to it. Even in real life somewhere he had defined roles for all of us and whether we accept it or not, we were performing to his tune.

He made you play your part well and made me play mine, what is the point in digging back. I cannot move on because I don't want to."

Greshma did not continue the discussion as it was taking things to a different level altogether. She knew deep inside her heart that all her life she had only performed to Master's instructions. Somewhere she was happy that he was no more, but she could not express that happiness. So, she politely took Neelakshi's leave and went to her room.

Greshma kept on thinking about Neelakshi's comments for some time and then said to herself, 'I need to get out from here, as soon as possible.'

She switched on the television. News channels were talking about Keval Kishore Rajput. There were some old photographs of him, which were used to share his journey into politics. Media of course knew just half the truth. Family photograph with his mother, father and son on one side and a single photo of Neelakshi on the other side were flashed on television. There was an arrow indicating, that she was to be a part of this family next year. Neelakshi stood as the most pitiable member amongst the five of them.

'Yes, life makes sure that you are at its mercy in some way or the other but I never succumbed ever,' thought Greshma.

She remembered how Neelakshi had changed after they went to Pune, in just three months. She went back to the old time,

*****

'Neelu had gone a little bizarre. She stopped talking to everyone, and most of the time was lost in her own world. Her behaviour was super unpredictable; just like a wildcat, she would pounce on anyone that she would come across. This happened when just a few days were left for Master, Bank and Dabbu to leave from Pune, after settling us.

'Last night' as Neelakshi used to quote it, we actually got to know the reason for her strange behaviour.

We all went to Fire and Ice disco, buying the most expensive ticket of Rs.1000 per person. This ticket was not sponsored.

It felt like an achievement. But since the alcohol was too expensive, we chose not to drink there and took our quota from home itself. We behaved sober despite being drunk, as we saw the bouncers not allowing drunken people inside.

When we went inside, we danced like mad to Simesh Savariya songs and our Scorpio Group was a part of 'SS Hate Club'. It was his birthday. The owner of the club was said to be his close friend and so he threw an 'SS Night'. The tickets were cheap for all the obvious reasons; they would have otherwise been 2000 per head on usual nights. *Daaru* can make you do anything.

After the last song we were all set to pack up, but Neelu was up to something unexpected. She kept looking at Master in amusement, for a long time. Within seconds her expressions kept changing and suddenly we saw her moving close to him, holding his hair tight, bringing his face down and giving him, a deep pink mark. That was too filmy, she did not stop nor did she get embarrassed.

A small-town girl with middle-class, conservative values shocked everybody including the guy himself. She was proud of having expressed her feelings in front of the world, for her even this was an achievement.

It was her moment and nothing and nobody was more important at that time. We were all drunk and could listen to a soft music of violins in the background, even when there was no music.

The whole sequence was longer than shown in Hindi films. I still remember her song for Keval –*Ye pal ye lamha, ye kal tha tanhaa*

Ye hal si mushkil, ye til si thandak

Jo chubh si jaye aur haule se mujhe kahee jaye

Ki main ho jaaun tere ishque mein fanaaha'

*****

'That was not love for sure; Neelu had something else in mind. They were behaving as if they both were on a dangerous plan against each other. Their relation was always complicated. They were always on a wild mission against each other and for each other. They cared for no one around. Probably that is the reason why she was still out of Keval's family frame.

How could Neelu be so expressive, she might have seen that honesty in Keval's eyes which I did not.' Greshma said to herself and went back to the old time.

*****

Next day at the railway station, just before the train left, Master went to her with a bouquet of flowers and chocolates.

Our dear girl again surprised us. She shouted in front of everyone, "Keval this is a very girlish way of expression; I did not expect this from you. Please be what you are.

Just tell me that I have chosen a very difficult person in life, tell me I need to think a hundred times before accepting your proposal, tell me you are crazy, tell me if still my decision is 'yes' then I would have to be ready for a lot of challenges, tell me that you are difficult to deal with, tell me you never know what all you may go through, tell me everything that would make my decision even more strong. For God's sake don't behave like usual guys, they suck!"

Oh God, her eyes burnt straight into his as she spoke.

Master grabbed Neelakshi through her hair, jumped onto the railway track close and closer to the train running on the parallel track, kissed her till *the time it crossed them, left her with a jerk and said, "Charas you are an addiction, tujhe wo dunga jo tunee kabhi socha bhi nahi hoga. I don't want your yes or no."*

He left her with us without even saying bye, and she was so happy about it. They dramatically declared themselves a couple and that drama still remains a topic of interest amongst people.'

*****

It was wild enough, but not enough for love. Love doesn't come that easy. I have travelled a long journey in search of those honest eyes which had love and trust for me. Today I am Mrs Shashank Sen Sharma, married to a man who has honest love for me in his eyes.

Socially, it seems so easy to be his wife. He proposed, and I agreed, but life has been far more than just proposing and accepting. It's not always a fairy tale.'

Greshma with tears in her eyes saw the message in her mobile phone. It was from Rajat; he informed that he was to reach there by next afternoon along with Shashank.

Greshma forwarded the message she received from Rajat to Neelakshi, just to keep her posted about the new guests who would be arriving the next day.

Chapter 7

The Shaping of the Destiny

The inner–self is calling,

Something is building and rest is falling

I am happy about the new feeling

I have taken my first step,

Now it's destiny that's taking shape, my darling

Greshma was a confident woman now; she needed no relation to define her existence. This strength came to her with time, as she acquired power.

She still remembers the first time, when she used power to get her work done.

*****

'When Master left, Neelu started facing problems pertaining to her inconvenient office route as it was not possible for anyone to drop her to office every day. She called for her vehicle but since it was not transferred.

Traffic *hawaldaars* used to catch hold of her whenever they saw the MP number plate and she would bribe them to save the *challan (fined)* money. She spent fifty bucks on petrol and another fifty on bribe almost every third day. She hated to get her tank full, as there was no petrol lock in her Kinetic.

To get us out of that problem, Master Mind gave a brilliant idea, and the executers of that idea were Shark and Shady. All I had to do was, give a photocopy of my Kinetic papers to Neelu. That was risky, and we were warned to never keep both the Kinetics in the same place.

Things went smoothly for a long time until one weekend when we all met out for dinner. The restaurant was not very far from our place so all of us came directly from office.

Shangri-La was famous as 'first date spot' amongst couples who began their journey some thirty years back. It still had its own charm. They kept a record of their guest's first date and used to wish them every year. Also, if guests wished to revive their old memories, they would book the same table for them. It was believed that the couples who met there had a long-lasting relationship. Even couples of the new generation who were serious about their relationship began their journey of never dying love from this auspicious restaurant. It became a pilgrimage for lovers.

But we were shameless enough, and chose this venue only because we could not afford an expensive place at the month end and moreover, it was the closest to home.

It was after a long time that we all had come out for dinner. Shady had received his confirmation letter, which was a reason to celebrate. Though the three musketeers were not with us, we spoke to them over phone.

We were all going home for Diwali and were missing our families very much. All were charged up after the good food coupled with 'ghar ki batein', until we saw a surprise waiting for us at the entrance of the restaurant.

Both the Kinetic scooters were missing from where we had parked them. The boys went out to look for them and we saw a group of cheap *Netaaji* type 'mitra mandal' (a non-statutory youth political cell) guys coming close to us. They spoke in local language coupled a rude tone. We thought they had stolen our only means of transport.

As it is Neelu was going through a difficult time with her Kinetic and, to add to that, this problem was a bit too much for her to take. She started screaming; "Oh god! This city is full of thieves. Where is my Kinetic?"

A dirty man from the flock barked like a dog; "*Pauleece mein di hai*".

"What? Are you mad?" I said, shouting at them.

I felt like giving him a slap as he spoke. He was spitting while talking. He was indeed a cheap fellow.

"*Oo Madamji ek tau chori upar se seena jori. Ye hamara ilaaka hai, hamare yahan easa kuch bhi hoga to hum kisi ko nahi chodenge. Chup chaap bolo unme se kaun si chori ki hai?*" said the dirty man in his equally dirty tone.

Now that was too much to take. How can we steal our own vehicle and who are they to say anything? Neelu shouted at him; "*Abe oo, koi chori ki gadi nahi hai… apni zaban samhal kar baat kar warna jaan le lungi.*"

It was always difficult to handle her; the Ms Perfect looks she carried always invited unwanted problems for her. She looked like an easy prey to people.

As we saw those people giving her dirty looks, our irritation level started to reach its peak. Shark shouted at her, "Stop over-reacting Neelu, and let us handle it properly, for God 's sake. We are going to the police station now."

"Again, police station, I am sick of collecting my Kinetic from police stations," she cried.

"No, Baby don't worry; you please don't utter a word. Shark, be with me and Shady you please take care of her and don't let her come into the scene," I said to them. *Raat ko about sade gyara baje (11:30 pm) the police chowki* looked like a haunted place. It was very dark there, and we saw weird people sitting at the entrance. These *hawaldaars* looked like rapists to me but knew that I had to be strong.

Though it was my first official visit to a *Police Chowki*, it wasn't a bad experience at all. I got back Neelu's Kinetic and learnt the *Guru Mantra* of 'Confidence' for life. I discovered that it is a weapon that everyone is scared of.

"Bhai sahib hum yahaan apni do gadi lene ke liye aaye hain. Abhi kuch log unko chura rahe the fir baki log bacha kar unko yahaan le aaye." Shark started off with his bundle of lies, aiming at the most sober looking policeman from the bunch of half sleepy, ugly looking guys.

They had a paunch; I could not believe my eyes. They are supposed to be the fittest people of all, but they were at their worst that night. I wondered how the public could feel safe under their security.

"Kaun si gadi Madam?" responded the most sober looking policeman to me on Shark's question.

"Do Kinetic hain. Un mein lock nahi laga tha, is liye log usko chura rahe the. Kuch logon ne bataya ki apke pass layee hain" I said taking the cue from Shark.

Hawaldaar replied in confusion; *"hamare paass do kinetic hain jinka number ek hi hai... usmein se ek chori ki hai... aaisaa humko pata chala hai."*

I tried to neutralize the situation by saying, *"Chori ki to koi nahi hai Sir... kisi ne number plate chura liya tha... aur galti se same number plate lag gaya..."*

Dirty man that he was, he said; *"Dono gadi ka paper mangta hai humko."*

Shark then decided to take over, *"Milega sahaab. Dono ka paper hai hamare pass. Galti se hua ye, aur kisi ka dhyaan hi nahi gaya. Aap chaheen to chassis number se check kar sakte hain."* I never thought Shark was that smart. Rascal that the *hawaldaar* was, he said; *"Apne ko kuch bhi check nahi karne ka hai. Ye to MP ki gadi hai, iska NOC kahaan hai?"* he asked as he saw the papers.

"Sahab iske NOC ke liye apply kar diya hai abhi tak aaya nahi hai." He said.

"Jab aaya nahi hai to tum isko road par chala kaise sakti ho?" the rascal asked me.

I fumed with anger as I knew *Meri Neelu ka office kitna dur tha; "Hawaldaar Sahab kaise chala sakti ho matlab? Office is twenty-five kilometre from our place, how else to go there?"*

"Bus chalta hai, tampoo hai, rickshaw hai, usase jao. Tum dusare gaaon se aaye log yaha par apne baap ka raj samajhte ho," said the idiot. It seemed as if he thought us to be a bunch of college going kids.

"We are working, you fool. Do you know how difficult it is for a girl to travel in your cheap public transport with men giving dirty looks? *Aur teen bus badalne padte hain* to reach her office. *Rickshaw ke liye roz paise nahin hain hamare pass. Koi rape karega tab tum aaoge kya? Jaan le lungi tumhari."* I blasted off at him.

Shark was looking at me amazed; even Neelu and Shady who were standing out got the hint of what was happening inside.

"Humkoo kuch nahi pata rule matlab rule. Kal aana tum log." He was scared and wanted to throw us out of the place.

"Oh Bhaiya, rule kisko sikha rahee ho tum... saalee tum log pachas pachas rupaiye mein to rule bechtee rehete ho... abhi tumko bhi rupaie sughanungi to tum bhi yahee karoge... saale sab ke sab choor ho." I shouted.

"Ooo Madam yahan par tumhari bakwas sunane ko nahi hun... ab tumhari gadi yahee rahegi... aur mein complaint lodge karunga..." he said.

"Aree bhaiya jaane do usko... wo pareeshaan ho gai hai isliye aaiasa bool rahi hai... bolo kitnae loge...?" Shark tried to settle the matter with money.

"Tumhari madam meri aukaat pachaas rupaiee ki bana rahi hai... main salaa hajaar se kam nahi lunga... aur agar bakwaas kiya na to chori ke saath, fraud ka complaint bhi lodge kar dunnga." He said.

"Ek baar wapas se bolna… tumhara naam kya hai hawaldaar," it was as if I got the chance.

"Kya bolna…?" asked that cheap hawaldaar getting scared.

"Tumhara naam… yahaan par hum sab kya tumko pagal nazaar aatee hain? Main press mein kaam karti hun, ye hai mera press card. Tumhara naam kal paper mein chapna hai," I said taking his picture on my mobile and looking at his facial expression I knew *utar gaya botal mein.*

"Tum Press se ho?" suddenly his tone of voice lowered.

"Haan," I said.

"To tumko pehele hi bolna chahiye tha na," he said.

"Kya booleen? Tum sab logoon ka maksaad ek hi reheta hai," I replied.

"Aree nahi madam main tumhara fine apni jeb se bharta hun," he said.

"Koi zarurat nahi hai. Mujhe ye batao hum is problem se kaise bacheen," Shark said.

"Aap ek kaam karoo… ek FIR likhoo ke iss gadi ke NOC papers kho gaye hain aur aap iske papers kam se kam ek mahine mein Maharashtra ka number le loge."

After the formalities he said, *"Madam isko apne pass hi rakhengi… jab bhi kuch hoga to ye police waloon ko dikha dengi… koi problem nahi hogi. Bass bina dar ke gadi chalaiyega… agar koi chupne ki koshish karta hai to wo dur se hi samajh mein aa jata hai. Aur haan dono gadi mein PRESS likhwa lijiye, hum log wo gadiyaan chod dete hain."* Not to mention, but the last line was the tip for all the fresh migrants.

'The Power of Media' worked for us; I suddenly felt powerful. No one would ever be able to touch me. I was a media person, a fearless Media person. We went home late, really late that night, almost morning. Thank God we were out of that disgusting PG Auntie's trap; there were no time restrictions… otherwise during such adventurous nights she would have rocked. Thankfully next day was off.'

*****

It was 11:30pm in the *Badi Haveli,* but Greshma could not sleep. She decided to take a walk outside, but Ramu Kaka stopped her, as it was not safe to be out late at night.

She stayed inside and went back to the days when they were all preparing for their first Diwali trip home from Pune.

*****

'It was Diwali holiday in everyone's mind. All of us had applied for five days leave; it was for the first time we realized that when you are employed, you earn your leaves.

We were to leave on Friday; Thursday was the only day left for us to do our shopping. *Ghar waloon ke liye* shopping from our first salary was a great feeling. Like everyone, the first thing that we thought of was nothing else but, '*Maa Ke liye sari.*'

When we went back after shopping, all started exhibiting them and suddenly we had tears in our eyes.

Shark is such an idiot; he just knows how to spoil the moment. "*Salaa iss khushi ke liye to duniya ka harr sitam kurbaan,*" He said.

And for the first time Shady was serious, "*Abee sitam kurbaan nahi hota hai teri hindi ki to… either make it duniya ki har khushi kurbaan or make it duniya ka har sitam sehe lenge…*"

Shady wrote a song dedicating it to all the mothers -

Maa, sabse uncha rahe tera naam

Tujhe koti pranaam

Tere haanth ka khanaTeri pyari si godh

Tera dulaar, tera laad

Tera mujhko lekar duniya se wo itrana

Meri galtiyoon par bhi natkhat sa pardaa girana

Mere liye wo papa se ladna

Tere liye sehe lun main hazaaroon duniya ke sitaam

Maa mere liye bass tu, tujhe Salam

Maa tujhe koti koti naman koti pranaam.

"Phew that was too emotional, we were crying our hearts out and that rascal Shady did not even want to let this moment go. He captured everything in a video and uploaded it on a social networking site... Within no time, we started receiving comments. He took credit for getting the real performance out of us.

Next day we went to office with our bags and left in the second half itself, reservations were not confirmed except for one and we were hardly bothered about it. We were told that TT or TC whatever they call him, *ko easily pata sakte hain*, we had heard a lot of stories where the Ticket Checker acts as a saviour in such a situation.

Not just him, even the pantry-wala, the coach-attendant are all very helpful in exchange of a few notes. This is where we came across the other level of corruption. Yes, it's only lazy, convenience freak people like us who encourage such things in the society. We are all to be blamed for creating reasons to be exploited.'

*****

Greshma was lost in her thoughts till her cell phone disturbed. "Hey Shark, till where have you reached?"

"Gresh I think will reach early in the morning, just called up to check if all is fine. Do I need to get anything? Somehow I just guessed you must have not slept."

"Ya, you are right. I could not sleep; Neelu is in a very different state of mind. This house has lost its charm without Keval and media is away only because of me."

"What state?"

"You come here and then we will talk about it. I can't say anything over phone."

"Okay, and when is Bank coming?"

"Tomorrow afternoon, he is coming along with Shady"

"Oh! has Shady already come to Bhopal from Mumbai?"

"Yes, he has."

"Is Neelu around?"

"No Shark, she has gone to sleep. She did not sleep since yesterday."

"Shark, all four of us have spent a really good time together in Pune, and that bond was far stronger than our college days. Away from home, we actually bonded like a family. Even before I started a family with Shashank, I knew what it meant. One look at me and you guys could just guess if there was something wrong."

"Of course, Gresh! *Par hua kya?*"

"She still believes that Master loved her. Shark I understand what love is, and I know what Master was, I have been with him in the...," and she could not continue it.

"What are you saying Gresh, I can't make the head or tail out of it?"

"Nothing Shark; do you remember the time when we were going home for our first Diwali?" asked Greshma quickly changing the topic.

"Of course, how could I forget that trip, it was such an adventure. You did so much of *Natak*. God only knows how from that stupid *nautanki*, you become the most celebrated journalist of the country – Mrs Greshma Rastogi Sen Sharma. To me you're still that same old Gresh. I don't see any difference."

"It's a secret Shark. If you say this to me again, next time during an interview I will screw your happiness."

"You know me, Gresh; I will lie to all your questions and make you put your foot in your mouth in front of your own camera in your own live show. I am not easy and you know that."

"I know you can even do that Shark, but trust me, now I believe that efficient liars are creative people because they are efficient at making people believe what has not transpired. That is an art and, with time, I have changed my definition of lies," Greshma said, and with a pause she continued, "Shark you will not be able to do that to me in front of my camera and my live show, I promise you that."

"Deal?"

"Yes."

"Next show *jaldi karna.*"

"Sure, Mr Liar. Good night now, come soon, let me sleep, else I will not be able to get up early," Greshma said, hung the phone and thought, "I have never slept with Shark, still there is something about him that gives me strange vibes and this is only after I left Pune," she slept after sometime.

Raj was not able to sleep; he was going to Keval's house after a very long time. Probably after that fight two years back, they hardly spoke at a personal level. It was only work that had bound them together and that too only because Raj was at such a senior level that nothing could pass through his table unnoticed.

And Keval had reached to such heights in business and politics that every day he or his referrals needed Raj's help on some issue or the other, be it related to land or industry or anything else for that matter. Raj never did anything for free, of course. For him Master was his Mentor, and he could never deny that despite being the most creative liar on earth.

He chose to travel by train, as he did not want to drive the road where Master died. While he was sitting next to his AC first class window, from where apparently, he could see nothing, he started thinking of their train journey when they were going home from Pune to celebrate their first Diwali

*****

'All of us reached the station a little *aage pichee*, not together as our offices were in four different corners of the city.

We felt as if we were Super Heroes, who were going back home after a lot of hard work. Though we could feel that the poison of the Scorpio was getting diluted with poison of life, but we knew no one could defeat us.

Shady and I were waiting for our pain, 'Gresh and Neels'. Neels was at reservation counter to check if our tickets could be confirmed. Gresh of all the people came with four bags. It seemed like she was all set to go and never return. With her usual fighter tone, she was arguing with the rickshaw wala– '*bhaiya main ek paisa zyada nahi dungi. Apko maine bola tha meter se station jana hai aur thoda luggage hoga uske dus rupaiye upar se dungi.*'

"What happened Gresh?" I went and asked her till she settled her luggage down.

Gresh replied to me then, "Shark, he is charging unnecessary money from me."

As a true gentleman, I offered her help; "Ok *tu chal* I will handle him, anyway your stuff is just too much. Either we would have to become *coolies* or you would have to shell out more money."

"Just shut up Shark, I will take my stuff one by one. You just be here." Gresh snapped back.

"Just shut up girl, you just take this stupid small bag and we will get the rest. Need to talk to you on this nonsense scene that you are creating here," I said.

"I don't want to Shark," she replied in her same irritating tone and left happily with the small bag. Girls are always *chalu*.

I was irritated by her behaviour and started complaining, as Shady and I took her luggage to platform no 4, "Just look at her Shady, God knows what she is up to? These girls are super crazy; it's so difficult to be friends with them for friend's sake. These girls behave as if we are their pseudo-boyfriends. I hate it Shady."

Shady was always a rascal. Even with those heavy bags he took his hands back to where his pony was fixed once upon a time, indicating that he was up to some mischief. He said, *"Tu piye ja do ghut khushi ke, issi bahane, kyun ki khoon ke aansoo rulane wali abhi aai nahi hai. Ye to padosi ki hai, abhi yeh hi nahi jhilti, sale toh jab teri aayge tab to teri khair nahi hai."*

I got pissed with him, "Shady you are a *haraamkhoor of first order. Saale kutte"* While carrying those big bags of bricks, I thanked god, for girls don't know what boys talk about them behind their back. We are all scoundrels and yes, we are. *Sala dost ki biwi ya girlfriend hi zyada achhi lagti hai.*

Neelu called up Shady and informed, "Boss I found out that there was no chance of getting our tickets confirmed. Diwali time means full pack trains. No TT will come to our rescue today, not even to check the tickets; they all know there will be no cancellations."

"Oye but will we even get a chance to sit?" cried Shady as Neels disconnected.

"I knew it dude. Just be ready for the most adventurous journey of your life. *Iss moti ke bags mein to lagta hai patthar pade hain,* they are so heavy," I said all drenched.

*****

Raj continued the journey back to his memories as the train moved ahead from the station and his neighbour switched off the reading lights,

*****

'Somehow, we reached the platform and discovered that there was some tussle between both our pains, as in girls.

God knows why I always love talking about girls, all my life after college I have slept with many, and knowing them was the last thing I bothered about, but somehow for my pains I always felt like a responsible father. I did not like to see them sitting poles apart."

Shady ran up to them to know what had transpired between them; "*Oye Neels kya hua? Tum dono pagal type kyun behave kar rahe ho?*"

"*Pata nai Gresh ko kya hua hai Shady.* She is talking weird," cried Neels.

I got really pissed now and yelled; "*Kya hua, ab kya bakwaas kar rahi hai wo?* Like a madwoman, she was fighting with that *rickshaw wala*. Now what is she doing with you? Has she started biting you?"

Dumb Neels replied in her irritating innocence; "Not yet, Shark. Do you know what, she says - that if our seats don't get confirmed we would have to pay her for sharing her seat, else we can find a place elsewhere?"

Listening to this crap, thankfully Shady did not react. Instead he said; "Relax guys. I think there is some serious problem with her. Let her say whatever she wants to. You guys don't panic as if, she has asked us to jump in front of a fast-moving train. Thank God we did not get into internet booking *funda, warna chalu ticket ki line mein lagna padta so alag, aur fir to AC mein ghusne bhi nahi diyaa jata.*"

We were lost in our discussion on the platform, until I realized; "*Oye train chalne lagi boss, time ho gaya.* Where is Gresh?"

"She is in. Let's get in fast," said Neelu.

"But why she did not call us?" said Shady as we were running to get in.

"Because she has gone mad," Neelu said jumping into the train as we helped her get in. All of us dived one after the other into the moving train. For Neelu it was not the first time.

"*Salaa bhaagte bhaagte train pakdi thi… seriously agar do second bhi late ho jaate to ho jaataa humaaraa Happy Bday;*" said Shady, trying to control his breath.

There she was sitting next to the window, on her reserved seat, with fellow passengers who had encroached the rest of the seat. It was so visible from their faces that they were without reservation.

Shady said; "*Shark kya bolta hai, tujhe bhi lagta hai na chehere dekh kar ki inke pass reservation ticket nahi hai.*"

"Of course," I replied.

"*To saloon ko maar kar baith jayeen kya?*"

Making him understand was a difficult task, so I had to say; "Please ok, you would not even have a place to stand if Gresh insults and throws us out. She does not seem to look in - friend in need is a friend indeed mood"

"Then what do we do?"

"Do nothing, just stand in front of her, if she asks for money in exchange of place to sit, we will give her, I am carrying some." I said proudly.

"*Raat ko to waise bhi* both of us would have to sleep down on the floor while both the girls would relax."

Suddenly Gresh got up and asked for tickets from them. One of the guys tried to act smart with her, and that gave us a chance to fight for the security of our darling friend.

"Then a few minutes down the line, the whole scene was completely different, *now* people without confirmed tickets felt jealous watching us sit comfortably beside our friend."

Shark smiled and moved the horses of his memories to the beautiful girl who wore a red top and denim jeans, as she passed by asking for the TT. 'Looking at that girl I excused myself from my group to attend nature's call.'

She was the first one and the only one whom I wanted to know without sleeping with.

That was the time when I was not aware of my talent.

The girl was beautiful, her name was Pooja Chauhan, born and brought up in Bhopal, and she did her Law from Pune. She worked with a law firm for one year and now was doing her MBA. One year younger to me and extremely magnetic, to the extent that she attracted me for my entire life and now enjoys all luxuries of the world as Mrs Pooja Raj Bhandari.

*****

Every day I try to release myself from her magnetic charisma, sleep with other women, and come to her with a feeling of victory. I hate her; she lied to me about her first affair.

The train stopped at a station, Raj thought of going down for a cup of hot tea, but then decided to dropped the idea and went back to his memories.,

*****

'We got a huge welcome at the station. Everyone had come to receive us, except Gresh's parents. Her father had not come to see her off, nor did he come to receive her when she was practically coming after six months. It was clear now that there was some serious family problem.

Funny thing was; that Shady's parents could not even recognize him without a pony; Aunty asked if he missed his train, when he was standing just next to me, she said, "*mera beta sudhar gaya wahaan jakar.*"

Master deliberately played that cheap song "*Mera Piya Ghar aaya*" in honour of his beloved. No one else knew about it though.

We got to know that people in the city were on a look out for fresh link up stories. These were for Siya's 'Link up Column', a weekly section in the city's growing daily newspaper *Sach*. She was a journalist who helped people enhance their skills at smelling the fragrance of 'Link up'. She brought many hidden love stories of famous and infamous people to light and became popular.

I knew for sure that since *Sach* was Master's product, even Siya's column must have been his brain child.

After having spent a good time with everybody home, finally the Scorpio Men planned some time out, together at our favourite CCD, next to Hotel Ranjeet. Master shared with us that with his father's help; he had done some investment in 'Sach News Paper' and was planning to expand the circulation starting from North MP. That is where I caught him "Link up, is your baby, right?"

Casually he said that it was a very small yet an important tool for future. He mentioned about some land problem that was going on in their native place, Pahargarh. His father wanted that land to build a factory, but his relatives had encroached it. Somewhere Uncle had dropped the idea, but not him.

Shady and Dabbu were busy watching birds, "After going to Pune I thought would lose interest in city girls, but they seem so fresh" said Shady. "Their sense of dressing has improved.'

Dabbu looked amused, "dude it's only we the NRBs (Non-Residential Bhopalis) who would understand this feeling. *Tu chill maar.*"

Shady behaved like a weirdo until a girl yelled at him. Disappointed he said, "That is the only reason why Pune girls are better."

But for me the girls were not important at all, I wanted to know something else from life. My only interest was in the next plan of action. My Bank job would have given me maximum one year of energy to survive but my greed was bigger.

Master knew what I was thinking, looking into my eyes he said, "Let's plan it big, brother."

I knew that within three months all the High Net worth Investors in Pune, would be my clients and in the next six months' time, the company would give me promotion

We people from central India are too good at talks, we grow up in a mixed culture, healthy environment and we don't have too much of financial burden. So, we are calm and that reflects in our conduct very well.

He continued, "I know dude, you are not made for small things, we will do something extremely big. I already have plans for you, will discuss in case you are interested."

He was careful with me in a war of words. It's not in good health for anyone to rub me the wrong way. Master knew if even he tried, he would be snubbed. Only I knew the secret of the cold war between him and his father.

Dabbu had done a lot of ground work for his project. Keval's father agreed to finance it, but he did not want Keval to interfere in it. Dabbu's uncle was also helping Keval in some project, but it was in its nascent stage.

Shady was somewhere unhappy with his work, he was missing his freedom.

The day before we were to leave for Pune, we got to know that Gresh was not coming along with us, and finally the whole story was disclosed to us.

Evening she called all of us to college canteen and said, "See guys, my father had a major loss in his business and is not in a sound state of mind. Everyday lenders come to our house creating an awkward situation for us. My company is in the phase of downsizing and a lot of people are losing their jobs due to some reason or the other.

The latest reason is reference check, where I am a hundred percent sure that I will be thrown out. It's better to be with my father at this point of time than being humiliated at work."

Somewhere I was happy that if Gresh was not coming, even Neel's family would not send her.

But Master somehow was very keen on sending them back with us. There was practically no reason for it. We knew he hated girls, but here we got to see a different side of him. He said, "Are you mad,

Gresh? Uncle would never want to be known as father of a loser, at least fight once before giving up. He has been through many ups and downs in his life and practically he knows how to handle them. *Jitna* I know of uncle, he will definitely fight back and come out strong. And about your stupid reference check, who said you don't have authentic documents? Has anyone said anything to you? Do you even know if your reference check is done? It's already done baby, and I had taken that call here."

Gresh replied like an idiot, "No one has said anything to me as yet, but I am sure once we are back from the holidays, our reference check will be done. I have heard a lot of stories about, what happens when people go back to work after their first long leave." She took a little pause, wore a funny expression and questioned him, "Are you sure my verification is done Keval?"

I felt like killing her. I never understood why girls are so confused and hyper. If they are not sure of their decisions then why do they declare them as 'National announcements'? That is the only reason I use them for only one thing and calm all their excitement down.

"Yes, I am telling you," said Master.

"Aur agar main pakda gai tau?" said the girl whom I hated the most at that time.

"Tau tera juta mera sarr, jo bolegi wo haarunga. Aur agar nahi pakdi gai tau?" Master said.

"To tu jo bole wo karungi," said Gresh.

"Pukka, mana to nahi karegi," said Master.

"Of course, not stupid," replied the ungracious Gresh. And it was finally decided that both the girls would be going back with us. And there crashed my happy dream with a *zoor ka jhatka*. All could hear the crash but I tried to hide the source of it.

Sunday all four of us we were sitting in our favourite living room in Pune home, lost in our own world. Suddenly silence broke when the doorbell rang.

"Your Pizza Sir," said a man to Shady as he opened the door.

"Who called for Pizza?"

"Are you mad who would call for Pizza, *itna sara ghar ka khana rakha hai?*" said Gresh.

"Please check the opposite flat, this order is not ours. Thanks," said Shady to the man, slammed the door and asked us, "What are you guys thinking?"

"About tomorrow," I said.

"About office," Gresh said.

"About my clients," I said again.

"About what time will I get up tomorrow," Neels said.

"About my boss," said Gresh.

"Strange no one said "home". It was clear we were both physically and mentally back and so were our worries. Whole night we were not able to sleep, we kept on pouring coffee in mugs one after another, biting nails, trying to complete presentations, making mail drafts, listing down pending jobs and doing what not. While we finished our work, we spoke about funny stories that we had collected from experienced people. Title was – 'joining after first official leave'.

- Shady shared about one of his senior's experiences who got to know that her company was to shut down and she would be jobless in two months' time.

- Gresh shared the incident she heard from one of her colleagues, who got a big firing on the first day. His boss had listed down points to prove that that his package was too high to take leaves.

- Neels senior's father made her resign on the phone because her boss had called her during vacation.

- Gresh shared another incident about her colleague she got to know that her boss had resigned so she was all free from everyday fights. She decided that she would make her terms clear to the new boss right from the first day.

- Shady shared another story of his colleague's friend who came back after travelling North India. He left the office on his first day of re-joining itself, to pursue his love for travel. He is now working with the National Geographic channel.

I had nothing to contribute and so only listened to these stories and enjoyed. Strange people, strange incidents but yes going back to office after the first official break was not an easy task It gives jitters, even if you are a very composed person. There is always a nagging fear.'

*****

Raj tried to sleep but somehow could not. It was the same restlessness that he felt many years back. That was when he wanted to confess to Rajat, on sleeping with the girl who came as his guest to the New Year's party.

*****

It was for the first time Shady had come with a girl; she was so hot. I could not resist and what happened was obviously something no friend would like. But she was very fast; she already eyed the guy who would drop her home after the party.

I owed a confession to Shady and apologized to him after one year. After that normal dialogues between us started and I was really happy. But today, there is much more to confess, but I don't know to whom.

Chapter 8

The First Step towards Success

This is all I could gather

To climb first step of success ladder

I knew it would come to me one day

For this, a heavy price I had to pay

Raj Bhandari woke up early in the morning and got down at the station, Rajput staff was already there to receive him; his name was written in bold "Mr Raj Bhandari", he knew it was Greshma to have done that, as he got into the car, he saw two small cushions at the back seat for him, he knew this was Neelakshi.

The driver who received him had been there for many years. He used to speak only in Bagheli till Raj (Shark) met him last; around four years back. Today he greeted him in English. There was a crude reality that connected them; it was the death of their source of connection, Keval Kishore Rajput. They were silent for a long time.

To break that silence, driver played some music and Shark could guess that it was Keval. He used to love Kishore Kumar and the basic reason why Raj and Keval got along well, was their love for music. Everything was so defined.

Raj asked the driver to switch off the music and began some conversation.

"Bansidhar why did you bring that board along, when you knew I am coming?"

"Sirji it was Greshma Madamji's order. I know you as *chote hukum's* fair friend. You came to *Badi Haveli* once. *Aaj pata chalaa aapka naam 'Raj Bhandari' hai.*"

Bansidhar slowly started giving Raj updates on *'Badi Haveli'* and their discussion moved to the unfateful night. By now he was speaking clear *Khadi Boli Hindi.*

With the ups and downs in his voice, Raj could make out the emotional trauma he was going through. "*Shahab maine bola tha Chote Hukum ko pooja ka prashad kha kar jao, maa khush hai, fir koi phone aaya aur wo ekdam sheher ki aur nikal gaye, aur saberee humko pata chala ki sab khatam ho gaya.*"

Raj was wondering; "who could have called up, there were many people though, but can a *'Prasad'* cause death? It was many years since I spoke to him. It was so difficult to forgive him and I still haven't."

As he was lost in thoughts, his cell phone interrupted.

"Good Morning Shark. How was the journey?"

"It was good and strange too. Not that I am a new guest to the Rajput's but everything seems as if I am here for the first time."

"Yes, I understand. Just come as fast as you can, please."

"Yes, Gresh I am reaching. How are Neelu, Maa Sahab and Little Kishore?"

"They are all fine, it's the second day and there is nothing hidden from you."

"Both you and Neelu remain with Maa Sahab."

"Yes, we are with her."

"What is the scene in the CM house?""I am yet to connect with Dabbu for the update, but media is going mad. They are creating stories which never existed. Janpad Party is planning to have a tie up with Lok Party which supporting Sach Party, just one day back.

Everyone is now trying their best to grab the chair. There is a chaos amongst the supporters and some people are conspiring to team against us at the core."

"Nothing is left Gresh; all our efforts have gone down the drain. Sach Party has become an orphan now. Despite playing a big role in making it strong, I feel so helpless. It reminds me of the time when Dr S. Prasad Mookharji expired unexpectedly, when CJP was just formed."

"No Shark, we will definitely see someone takes charge, the party has won, five years execution plans are ready. Master did everything before he left."

"What about us Gresh?" he said in a deeply hurt voice, as if he survived becoming a handicap, after a failed suicidal attempt.

"Something would definitely work out Shark. I spoke to all the heads of key political parties who supported us, and they are still with us. Actually, they don't have any option. If they go elsewhere, all their dark deeds would come to light and even the investors would kill them."

"Gresh, you mean Master played his game, even with them?"

"But his calculation worked well for everyone Shark. In the process, we have all gained. The web that he created; would not let us lose that easily."

"Are you mad Gresh, what about mental peace? You can't even imagine all that I have done to make him reach till the CM chair," said Raj and disconnected as he knew the conversation would lead to a direction where he would have to open a lot of un-open cards.

Car passed the crowd, all clad in white clothes. Greshma came out to receive and escort him to his room. He was supposed to share his room with Rajat. After so many years they were to become roommates again. He met Maa Sahab, who had just returned after meeting people. There were some politicians who suggested her to join politics but she remained quiet. Shark touched her feet and kept quiet.

"*Beta* Raj, it's a difficult time, but I don't want you all to sit and sulk. There is a lot to be done; Keval and his father have made it really big. They left everything for you all to carry on and I am sure you will respect that. I look at this Little Kishore, as our future. Please have breakfast and rest, Shashank and Rajat will be here by afternoon it seems," said Maa Sahab.

Surprised at her words he looked at Greshma and gave an expression which meant, that her practical side proves, that only she can be Keval's mother. A woman; who wouldn't give up even in such a critical time.

"What happened to Maa Sahab Gresh?"

"I don't know, and that is why I said that we will discuss once you are here. Even Neelu has become mad, staying with her. She says that she would accept Neelu as her daughter- in- law in front of the whole world."

"Meaning what? Is Keval alive?"

"No Shark, she will declare her as wife to his dead son. She would confirm herself as witness to a marriage which never happened."

"Why?"

"She wants a caretaker for her grandson and Neelu is a perfect fit, so emotionally she is trying to trap her. There are a lot of things she is conspiring in the dark, and Neelu is unaware of everything."

"This mother and her dead son would make us mad. Gresh I now feel that, it was a wrong decision to come here."

Mobile phone call interrupted their conversation, and it was Shashank (Bank) calling his wife Greshma to inform that they had left early in the morning but would be late since their car broke on the way.

"I don't know Gresh, it just stopped in front of that spot, and I could hear Master scream," said Shashank.

"What? Are you and Shady fine?"

"Yes, Gresh, and don't worry, we will reach there by 2:30pm."

Greshma looked a little disturbed as she disconnected. "Shark, I hope all settles soon. Not that I am scared of death, but it's still hard to believe what it does. Are you sure Keval is dead?"

"I have not seen his body Gresh, but there was something strange that did not allow me to come by road," said Raj.

"Do you believe in ghosts, Shark?"

"As much as we exist, even they must be. Well, I term them as the unknown, to be very precise. Are you scared of them?"

"Even if it exists Shark, I am not scared of them or for that matter anyone."

"*Achha* this driver was talking about some '*Prasad*' story."

"Yes, there is a belief amongst people that one should not do *Pooja* at all or should perform it properly. One must have Prasad, spend the night in the temple and then leave next morning. People feel that he disobeyed the law, so had to bear the consequences.

Since she is their family goddess, the whole family had to suffer the consequence. Maa Sahab also believes in it. When she got to know about it, she distributed *Prasad* to everyone and even kept it beside both the bodies. She did another *Pooja* to apologize for Keval's mistake. She feels that it would be a bad omen for Little Kishore otherwise."

"But that is strange Gresh how is it possible? Master had been fighting to educate these villagers and get superstition out of their mind. Despite being his mother, Maa Sahab believes in all this."

"Whatever we say, Shark; that woman has lost her son and her husband, and nothing in the world can bring them back. Just as you believe that unknown exists, for them it could be this belief that exists," said Greshma and left for her room.

She called for some coffee. Neelakshi was not feeling well, so she slept till late. Greshma went back to her old days as she sat with her cup of coffee.

*****

'I got my first appraisal and promotion one and a half years after joining. Soon I was to get an opportunity to work with politics and crime division. There was a forum my company was creating for social awareness and reader involvement.

Having worked in the marketing division helped me understand the pulse of the reader, and my Journalism background made me a perfect fit for that new profile.

When I spoke to Master Mind, he encouraged me to look at exploring an opportunity in journalism itself. I had almost forgotten about my first love, but somewhere his words brought back that lost fire in my belly.

I was the last one to get the appraisal, rest all got it within one year of their joining. I was looking forward to my chance, but it's just that everything good comes to me after a long wait. It comes almost at the time when I have lost all my hopes.

To my surprise, the topic of appraisal opened some old wounds. Shark was dissatisfied with his appraisal, "*Yaar pura khoon chusne ke baad bhi* I got such a poor growth, but you are lucky Gresh. I felt like joining some underworld gang and give my boss's *supaari*. If she weren't a woman, I would have shown her what it is to mess with me."

And even Shady was not happy with his appraisal, "You know what, Shark *salaa mera kutta boss, ladki ko mujhse double appraisal deta hai*. He feels that girls are more deserving and believes in woman empowerment. *Saale ne puri duniyaa ki auratoon ka theka liya hai*. I am shocked the way he treats us dude, like jokers. The whole day they gossip, by evening they leave all the pending work on us. And next day they take full credit for the complete task."

"Then why do you do their work, dude?" said Neelu.

Shady pounced at the opportunity to answer; "The way they come, any man if he has a dick would not say 'no'. You don't even know how these girls are, whether they are small town *chipkalies* or a metro butterflies, they all are the same."

I said, "Guys, you really need a girlfriend now."

I was seething with rage from inside. How these guys could talk so loosely about girls. Shark saw me and tried to cover up for his words "*Oye tu to senti ho gai yaar.* Chill, we did not mean anything. It's just a way to let out. *Tu bhi chaar gali de de.* It feels really good. Try it."

I tried to control my tears as there was no point in stretching the topic, we were aware of the level, this conversation could go to.

Post my appraisal we were all at the same level, still were way behind our dreams. Shark could still only think of buying expensive cars, but had managed enough savings to buy a second hand car.

There was a ground to stand, we were not empty handed yet, there was an urge for abundance. We were on the first step of Success Ladder.'

*****

It was past 10:30 am and Greshma had to get ready, as she was supposed to help in the kitchen. She got out of her bed and went to the bathroom.

Chapter 9

A Friend in Need

You were with me when hope was broken

The smile on my face is our friendship token

For what you had given

Nothing better can be given or taken

Raj engaged himself with Little Kishore, 'This kid is positive and really bright, unlike his father.' He was happy to see Little Kishore as an intelligent kid; he was sharper than his own kids.

He played with him for some time, till he received a call on his cell phone; he did not want to pick up the phone but had no other option.

"Raj, Mehta here."

"Mehtaji, good morning."

"I don't think it's a good morning for me, Raj. I had to cancel my Europe tour and come back when I got to know about Keval's news."

"Yes Mehtaji, it's a big loss for the state."

"I am not much interested in anything else, but my project."

"I understand, Mehtaji. Even I am figuring out things; please give me a little time."

"Raj, are you sure Mehta and Sons will get the MP Road Development contract? Based on your words and scope of work, we have invested a lot in building more assets and Sach Party. If I don't get this contract, I will come on the road."

"Don't worry Mehtaji, trust me, have I ever let you down in last six years of our friendship?"

"That is the only reason I invested on your single request, Raj, otherwise I would have not."

"Don't worry, I am out of town for next two days, will meet you once am back in town."

"Ok, see you then. Bye" and he disconnected the phone.

After sometime, Little Kishore went to play with his friends, leaving Raj alone with old memories. Raj once again was back to the old days,

*****

'Gresh was almost in tears the day she got her first appraisal. It was such a typical girlish behaviour which irritates me to the core. They don't know how to handle jokes, yet want to dive into a conversation. It's difficult for men to keep a track of their mood swings.

After some silly conversation, we decided to go out to celebrate. The celebration got disturbed when Master Mind called up, to inform that Shady's father tried committing suicide and was in the hospital.

We at once rushed to the station and when we reached, Shady said, "*Boss Shark tu katle ab*, I will be going home on whichever train is available."

"Dude, I am coming with you; we will get a direct train from Manmaar Station, I'll drop you till Habibganj station and come back on the next train, as it is *kal Saturday hai*."

It was not easy to convince that rascal. As we went inside the station I wondered about the significant role, that railway stations play in 'The Scorpios' life. Whenever there is a dramatic turn, we find ourselves standing at the station.

Keval had come to pick us at Habibganj station; he rushed us to the hospital. Uncle had taken loan to send Shady's elder brother to the US, some 13 years back for higher studies. There was a huge age difference between both the brothers.

After reaching the US, *Bhaiya* met with an accident and died on the spot. Uncle could never get over his death. Though not much of the loan amount was left, but it broke uncle at this age.

Shady could never fill that gap in uncle's life. He did not know his brother much, but all he knew was that he had to make a lot of compromises all his life, since his father had huge debts to pay. This made him a difficult child, but he had deep love and respect for his parents.

I never saw my tiger this weak, but on seeing his father in that condition he broke. "I don't think I would ever be able to take his place in their lives ever, but I can't see Papa in this state either. I just want to pay off this disgusting debt and take my parents out of this hell."

Practically, I had nothing to say. At the most his parents could stay with us in Pune, but in no way could I help him with the debt money. I was myself struggling hard to save money for a second-hand car. And I did not have any courage to lie that day.

In this tragic situation, Master Mind emerged as a true friend; his strength was that could always connect with people, at the most needed time "Relax Dude. The debt amount is not big, Papa has already paid it, and when you have enough, you can pay it back to him."

I was impressed. There was no need for Master Mind to support Shady financially, but for friendship, he did. He encouraged Shady to look for a career of his interest.

I never used to speak to Master Mind on work front, we had difference of opinion and I never did whatever he suggested. Shady was succumbing to his philosophy on career once again. I stood there listening to the conversation as a quiet spectator.

"Dude you need to do what you are born for," said Master Mind.

"Meaning?" asked Shady.

"You are born to spread smile, not to sulk. This 10:00 am-6:00 pm job is not for you, rather I would suggest try your luck in television. There is a lot of scope."

"Are you crazy Master Mind, do you think this is a time to talk all this?"

"This might not be the right time, but it is not a bad career option. When you know your strength why you are still stopping yourself from exploring it? Somewhere you are killing yourself and committing a crime."

"It would be such a big risk. Who would pay for my luxurious in struggling days?"

"Money comes by itself dude, you yourself would have enough."

I did not understand why he was pushing Shady on pursuing a new career; in the process, he also gave his own examples.

"There is this land in our native village Pahargarh, that is encroached by my relatives. I went there to resolve the issue, because my father wanted to set a factory there, but guys, it's not that easy. My newspaper *Sach* is struggling for survival, getting more money from *Dau Sahab* is next to impossible, he has already invested enough.

I am working hard to raise money and there are many options. That land parcel has the potential to become a complete Industrial Zone. I am just figuring out how to get it done. So, relax, just take a risk. You have already taken it once, by moving out of Bhopal, and it paid off well. But you can't get stuck to one place, you need to move on."

I was surprised after seeing this side of him. He did not speak about any 'Game Plan' and was behaving like a human, but he did give signals of what was going on in his mind. Master had to attend some press conference in Mumbai the next day. It was organized by his father, in honour of his friend, Dr Bijoy Babu's book 'India and Future'. He was an internationally acclaimed Economist and Socialist.

Dr Bijoy belonged to the same native place as Master and was in UK for 32 years.

It was decided that Shady would stay with his father for a few more days, and Master invited me to join the next day's press conference. You never know when a new opportunity knocks on your door, so I agreed.

Chapter 10

A New Horizon

When you feel stuck for some reason

Sit, think and then act in a different direction

Every action reaches you to a new horizon

Raj was not the kind who would surrender easily. Both Keval and Raj knew that they needed each other, and together they were capable of doing any herculean task. But they never admitted this truth, ever. There remained a silent understanding that played a big role in their achievements, since the day they discovered this secret.

He was hungry but did not feel like calling for anything to eat. He kept himself engaged with the memories of old days. His thoughts took him back to the Press Conference in Hotel Lalit, Mumbai,

*****

"After launching his Book Dr Bijoy spoke about the potential which lies within the Indians and Indian Economy.

World Economy was facing an all-time low, and the Presidents and Prime Ministers abroad were making things difficult for the Indian migrants. They knew Indians with their hard work and focused efforts are capable of wiping out the locals from their own Economic System.

They don't mind paying 40% of what they earn as taxes, contributing their bit for the survival of the locals, and thus making them lazier. We have an unidentified potential to rule the world, but our political leaders' keep us busy fighting for our square meal and basic comforts. It's as if they fear that the table could turn anytime.

He quoted one of the Prime Ministers; "I have made things difficult for them to survive here, but we will not be able to fight the recession unless my countrymen feel the same fire." India was always and will always remain the 'GOLDEN BIRD' is what Dr Bijoy meant.

He said India is the future and if we don't discover our own capabilities, no one can help us. He gave an example of *kasturi mrug*, who keeps running all over the jungle, searching for the source of that lovely smell, without realizing it's in his own navel.

We Indians keep running abroad, forgetting that the major potential is here in our very own country. He spoke about Brain Drain along with the world recession.

He mentioned that the fear to secure for a better future compels us to save for the rainy day. He mentioned that we Indians don't have a habit of living a lavish life and somewhere 'not over spending is in mind'.

It's just that we don't realize that this is 'saving'. It is said about us that we live like the poor and die rich.

He said that we are a country of entrepreneurs; our economy doesn't run on pseudo-money; however, we need to believe in ourselves first.

He requested Media and PR agencies to start talking about "No recession in India".

This first session with Dr Bijoy was an amazing experience for me until I got to see his real face. It was no different from the teeming, insecure population of India. He always demanded a big cut in the investment done by his sources in the industrial zones.

Master Mind introduced us, but Dr Bijoy soon became my friend and partner in crime. I never liked the fact that his share was more than mine, yet we enjoyed each other's company.'

*****

Suddenly Raj heard some noise that ended up distracting him, "*Kaun Hai?*"

It was Ramu Kaka with a new servant; "*Kuch nahi Hukum naya hai banda, ulta khol reha tha darwaza, gir gaya. Aap ko kuch chahiye?*"

"*Nahi,* thank you," Shark said and went back to thinking about Hotel Lalit where they were through with the conference. Just about when he could locate Keval, he saw him bumping into one of India's biggest Business Tycoons, Mr Susheel Jeethani.

*****

"Ooops Sorry Sir, I did not see you coming. Let me get your bag," said Master, but I knew that it was a deliberate move.

The Tycoon did not seem happy with it.

Master took a little time in collecting the files that had fallen down; "Sir your report, it seems like you were trying to analyse it. If you ask me, I would suggest you focus more on your Factory 2, in MP, as it has not been explored to its full potential."

Angry old man curtly said; "What?"

"I mean, I am sorry Sir, but it was just my suggestion. Unfortunately, I have a sharp memory; it registers everything in split of a second," said Master shamelessly.

I just thought it was the last day of our life and Mr Susheel Jeethani would get both of us killed by his bodyguards. But still he patiently replied; "That's impressive, you self-praising boy, just in case you have a name."

"Sir, I am Keval Kishore Rajput."

"Mr Rajput it was nice meeting you, have a nice time and keep focus to yourself too. By the way your fly is open, unless you know what the whole world knows about me, I am a gay."

That was enough for me to jump into that stupid conversation. "We are sorry Sir; your time is more precious." I took Master in a corner; "You idiot, what are you up to? Why are you acting over smart?"

I haven't slept with any man in my life, and at that time I was just praying to God for a blissful escape as I saw a black man nearing us, "Mr Keval Kishore Rajput?"

"Yes."

The Black man, with a scary beard and deep dark ugly looking eyes, smiled at us and as he spoke his sparkling white teeth were clearly seen. I just thought he would eat Master Mind up. "Sir, Mr. Susheel has asked you to join him for coffee, in case you are free."

Master for sure had all the time in this world for this invitation, "Sure. It will be a pleasure. I'll join him in ten minutes."

I got really pissed at him, "Dude, you have gone mad and you don't even know what danger you are putting both our lives into. I don't think you are a gay, and if you are, then I don't know you from today."

"Just shut up dude and join me, I assure you, your *izzat* would be safe. You will not be raped by a man, at least not him and surely not in my presence. Nor am I a gay. He is such an important man, dude. Remember, I was talking to you about a big plan for you. He is the current chairman of AIC India and MP comes in the North Zone."

That was enough for me to join Keval, but the fear inside me still remained. We went there together and in chorus we said, "Hello Sir." To my surprise the reply from the other side was curt no more.

There was a bus that I was supposed to take for Pune, that evening; there was a job that I was to attend the next day. There was a respectful life, in which many girls were to have sex with me, but all the dreams seemed to collapse, as he looked at us and said, "Hello, Mr Keval Kishore Rajput." with a smile.

He continued, "If I am not mistaken your father is Mr Kishore Keval Rajput and your grandfather, was Late Shri Keval Kishore Rajput, from Pahargarh, MP, you have cement plants in Satna and your family is into construction business."

My dude was all prepared to become his dinner, "Yes Sir and my son would again be named Kishore Keval Rajput. That is how it works in our family."

The Gay Monster replied over-enthusiastically to this, "That was just like your father, my son, I like it. I have met both your father and your grandfather."

Master was out of control now; "And even to me Sir, when I was a child. Seven years old."

Gay Monster knew that his prey was effortlessly falling into his trap, he said smiling; "Oh you still remember that small meeting. We had come over to your place for dinner. That was my first visit to MP; we were planning to put up a factory there."

Master started sending wrong signals, "Sir I have shaken hands with you as a child. How could I forget that?"

The spark in the Monster's eyes was making me feel like running away from both of them, and letting them be with each other, for the next action; at least I would be safe. He replied, "That's really nice of you Keval. Your father is an amazing man and a dear friend.

So how is your work going? Am sure you must have joined him since you were in school. He used to proudly mention in our meetings that he wanted to see you as the most successful businessman in the country."

Thank God uncle was brought into the picture. Whatever Master felt about his father, I am grateful to him for that night. If not for him the fire between those two men would have blown the top of the roof. Though it was only for a little while, but it did pour cold water on Master's enthusiasm. In a little broken voice, he replied, "Yes Sir, I joined him very young, but... My father is never really happy with my work."

The Monster became calmer and replied in a serious tone then, "That is a Rajput trait my dear, even your father had to go through it. Don't worry, it will only improve you. Your father's only weakness is that he does not have good political connections, and that makes him miss a lot of good opportunities. It makes him look arrogant in the world of business. If you can get that right, nothing can stop you from fulfilling his dream."

Master Mind smiled at him; as if he received the biggest tip of his life, from none other than the Business tycoon himself. Somehow, I started realizing how important this meeting was.

Mr Susheel seemed to be extremely happy after meeting Master Mind; as if he had met his own son. He wanted to share every possible secret of his success with Master Mind, and did not get irritated even with my presence. Probably that is how mature people behave.

The tycoon went on sharing his business and life philosophy for over an hour. He said; "Being an entrepreneur has a huge responsibility attached to it. You are always the last priority, and the feeling that you contribute to happiness of so many lives is really great. You want to touch the lives of more and more people. Business automatically fetches profits; most important is your action and the philosophy behind it."

As he went on speaking my trust in him kept on building and so did respect for him. My fear had almost vanished by now.

The proud business tycoon shared; "Now my family is really huge, with over 10000 employees, 5 lakh shareholders, over 5000 vendors and business partners, with 80% retention and many crores of end consumers. Your scale to measure success automatically changes with your experience. It moves from monetary gain to the trust that you gain. You automatically grow."

"Vendors?" asked Master.

"Yes, my son, every single person who touches your life is important. Not just your raw material supplier or your Bank even your *paperwala, chaiwala, electricity meter check karne wala*, postman, driver, everyone is important."

It was hard to believe that a person of his stature lived his life to such details. He was so happy sharing an incident; "My newspaperwala's son, has now become an IAS officer, but since his father has retired, every morning the son comes to meet me with newspapers. We discuss politics and business over a cup of tea. He is my tea partner; sometimes we even play tennis together. He knows what he is, and he knows I would never mention about my role in his life."

Deeply impressed, I just jumped into the conversation without even thinking once; "Thank you Sir, you have made my life." Though it was distracting, but even I needed an introduction. Master Mind politely said; "Sir, he is Mr Raj Bhandari, my best friend. He is very sharp and extremely good at building relations. I was just suggesting to him to join the Associate of Indian Corporate. It will not only give him a good exposure but also…," and he paused for a while.

The White understood the Dark and without any hesitation, Mr Susheel said, "And it will help you in all ways Keval. Raj it will be a very good exposure for you, not just that, you will learn how to build and use power soon."

The whole conversation changed its track and also changed my opinion about a lot of things, now I wanted to become a part of it and buy latest first handcars. It was Audi in my mind first.

As Mr Susheel's Business Mantra went on he said, "I never waste a minute on people who are not capable of giving me anything or taking something sensible from me.

"That was it; trust me I felt like kissing him and at that time would have not even minded becoming a gay. Yes, he was tall, fair, and handsome. Even at the age of 70, he walked straight and did not need spectacles. He had a classic taste in clothes. Everything about him was sophisticated.

His next tip was very important. There is always a price for everything, be it our ambition. The bigger the ambition the bigger is the price. He suggested that one should always strike a balance between our personal and professional life.

Giving his own life experience he said, "I evolved in my thoughts as an entrepreneur much before time and devoted my life to work. My wife could never understand my philosophy; she left me and got married to a very simple man. Now she is in the US with my kids and they handle their step-father's small business, without any complaints. Professionally he is not a successful man, but personally he has everything because he made his family happy."

His next tip probably was for Master, "Being a business owner, you are bound to be emotionally attached to your work. This is not the right approach. You need to get good executors. They are functionally involved in your day to day work, hence capable of bringing out the expected results far better than you. While choosing such people, do take inputs from your father, I would not hesitate in admitting that I have learnt these skills from your father and he inherited it from your grandfather."

That was too much to admit for a successful man like him. I would have never been able to do that if I were in his place. Mr Susheel became my Guru since then. I had an urge for money but he taught me the way to route it respectfully.

Master Mind introduced me to him, and I was thankful to Master for giving a new direction to my life. I did everything possible under the sun in gratitude, but he back stabbed me in the Industrial Zone project at the last moment. It was important to take revenge for my mental peace and *that is the reason I wanted to kill him.*

Though I went to Pune that evening but knew my next destination and started working plans in that direction. Even I am good at planning.

For two days after the Press Conference we waited, but there was no news. Irritated with media behaviour, Master called up the agency person to know why the news did not get its due coverage.

Feedback that he got was strange, Media was a little hesitant in carrying the, 'No recession in India' bit, as it did not have a backup from any Indian bureaucrat. The statement was from an NRI.

Master lost his mind and decided to take charge of the situation himself. With the help of Mr Susheel, he got in touch with Mr Shirish Rajpal, Group Editor of *The Times of Hindustan*. Since the pressure was from Mr Susheel, their biggest client, he could not refuse. The article was published in a very positive and scientific way.

'It said, a ray of hope is seen somewhere in the dark and then moved on to what is going on in the world Economy. It informed about the way different countries were fighting with their status of Economy. Subtly it spoke about strength of India, taking extracts from Dr Bijoy's speech.

The article spoke about the need for Post-Office, to get recognition as a Bank. Lot of positive things that supported the 'No recession in India' bit were weaved in.

Article also spoke about the important role that our education system played in building aspirants. It stressed upon the need for Indians to take up entrepreneurship. The article said we have to realize that we have money and the potential to build opportunities. It also stated that it was time we take politics in the right spirit and tolerate no nonsense.

The article had small inputs from readers and spoke about the way small towns were growing.'

Once this article took the lead, suddenly there was a wave of articles talking about the same thing. Every big and small journalist wanted to add a personal flavour and present the same news in a different way. It was nice to see 'brighter side of the coin'.

After a positive response, the editor of *Times of Hindustan*, Mr Shirish Rajpal had become good friends with Master.

*****

There was a knock on the door again, *"Apko khane par bula rahe hain hukum,"* said the new servant of the family.

As Raj looked at him, he remembered the "push and pull" theory, over which Pooja and he would fight. It used to start from a dumb conversation, move to cheap discussions and then end with action.

"Ji hum aatee hain," he said and went to the dining room.

*****

All the five friends joined for lunch, Shashank and Rajat had already arrived.

As he saw everyone together, Raj suddenly seem to have lost his senses, "What are we all doing here, why are we not where we should be?

Gresh the news articles that were supposed to be handled by you, are screwed up by those inexperienced journalists.

Neelu there is a lot on the plate and you a sulking here, for god knows what.

Bank there are so many investors in the pipe line but you are here.

Shady your words make sense to people, but instead of taking charge of the situation, and making the most out of it, you are here.

And I like an idiot am hiding from the truth, as if I have all time in the world to mourn."

Greshma knew where Raj was coming from and it was important for her to calm him down, "Shark, there are lots of things under cover. If we take charge in haste, we might hit a wrong button and all the hard work would go down the drain. Calm down please, everything will be in our favour."

*****

A game is never one sided, once set, you need to wait and watch for the other player to respond. He also has strategies against you, and without patience you cannot understand the depth of the opposition, even if it is destiny.

They were eager to decide the next action plan, Keval made a lot of plans, one against the other and one supporting the other, but he never realized that there could be no plan against Death.

Chapter 11

The Turning Point

Many days we surrender

At times for good, but mostly for blunder

After deciding we sit and wonder

Why does it rain only after thunder?

Shashank had come to Pahargarh after a very long time. He was quietly listening to Greshma and Raj's conversation. Greshma was sitting on the dining table just in front of him, avoiding any eye contact.

The dining table was huge; it could accommodate twenty-four people. Just by the look of it, one could make out that it was an expensive table. A classic piece of wood rested on four beautifully designed two feet high pillars. The décor of the room and food gave a royal touch to the meal, and in every way made people feel not just special, but very, very special.

Shashank also felt good sitting in that room, but it was difficult for him to take this attitude from Greshma. He made several attempts to break the silence between them, but failed.

Greshma excused herself from the group and went inside the kitchen. The door of the kitchen was artistically designed; there was a beautiful serving window which was surrounded by a thin line of golden leaves from all the four sides. One could see a person passing from that window, as he entered the kitchen door to go to the main cooking area. Shashank's eyes followed Greshma; he could see her entering the door but did not see her passing through.

Raj meanwhile took over the discussion, "You must hear the English accent of the servants, and you will be surprised. The whole place has turned around 360 degrees after becoming the Industrial Zone. The land rates have gone up and so have the construction rates."

Greshma had been a witness to the growth of Pahargarh. After she joined 'Sach Newspaper' her journey to becoming the most celebrated journalist of the country passed through these roads of Pahargarh.

After completing two years of work, with Pune Media house, Greshma was sure that she would not continue, if they did not shift her to Crime division as a journalist.

As expected, they did not agree and she decided to quit the job, incidentally Keval was planning to expand 'Sach Newspaper' with the launch of Gwalior edition, which covered news from North Madhya Pradesh. His Indore and Bhopal editions were already launched and after Gwalior it was Jabalpur on the cards.

If everything went according to the plan, in following two years' time there were plans of launching a national news channel too. The growth plan was good and so were the career opportunities.

Keval offered Greshma an opportunity to work with *Sach* and suggested that if she wanted to pursue her career in journalism, she could consider it as her launch pad. He informed her that Mr Shirish Rajpal; Group Editor of *The Times of Hindustan* had agreed to mentor *Sach*, and she would get to learn a lot from him.

It was like a dream come true for her; she agreed to the proposal.

Greshma joined everyone at the table and taking clue from the discussion, went back to the time when she decided to join 'Sach Newspaper'

*****

After I got the job offer for *Sach*, I did not wait and immediately submitted my resignation. Everyone was shocked. I was known for taking impulsive decisions, but this one could have proved dangerous. Bank had completed his studies and was ready to marry me, but I gave him two more years.

My parents were happy with my decision of joining Sach. Papa thought that they would get to see me more often, and using my regular visits as an opportunity, he would get me to meet guys. As soon as my horoscope matches with any of the prospective Rajput bachelor, he would quickly settle my marriage.

It was decided that I would be shuttling between Mumbai and MP for at least two years. In Mumbai I was supposed to work as a trainee under Shirish Sir and sharpen my skills in both print and TV journalism.

I was to travel across *Sach* offices in MP to understand the markets before taking charge of the print division. Once trained in print, was supposed to take charge of other divisions.

Initially I was surprised when Keval offered me this job; he knew very well that I was to shift with Shashank to the US. He gave me a sarcastic reply, "Shashank will settle in the US only if I will let him Gresh."

"What do you mean Master Mind?"

"Nothing dear, I was just joking. Since we have Shirish Sir on board, I need a trustworthy person. Who could be better than you? There could be a fake bond which you might have to sign. But that is only for him, from my side you are free," he replied to cover up his sarcastic remark. But now I know it was all part of his plan.

Breaking this news to Neelu was very difficult; we were both dependent on each other away from family. It felt as if I was ditching her, but later realized that Master Mind had already worked out a plan for her. In last one and a half years, she started managing placements for CEO and other senior levels. With this experience she was suggested to move to a renowned PR agency in Mumbai.

The only difference was, that I was going to relatively known place and she was moving to the jungle. We were parting our ways without realizing that it was a game.

My first day at Gwalior office was an experience in itself. Gwalior covered entire news of North Madhya Pradesh, including interesting stories from the Chambal Ghats.

The ravines there are famous as homes to many dacoits, who have strange stories behind their new identity. In the so-called urban cities, one can't let one's extreme self out. Even the protests here are meant to be organized.

If one really wants to challenge the existing system, he is free to join the parallel system but there was no place for a third system, it only exists in The Chambal Ghats.

I went to Gwalior by train, unaware of the new episode that destiny had planned for me. It gave a new perspective to my way of thinking. I met someone special there.

I was driven to the guest house in a car which had PRESS written on it. There was a room booked for me already. It was a scary place. For the first time I went for an out-station job, all alone.

The room was decent, but after leaving the hectic, yet glittery life of Pune, I felt very low there. I thanked God that Mumbai was on agenda. Thoughts of being raped started haunting my mind, as I realized that I would be staying alone in that room.

It took me a while to come to terms that this was just the beginning of a new adventure and there were many more to come. Sometimes it is good to act before thinking, because when we think we try to be more cautious of results and bind our actions. This dilutes the thrill of the task. I was wondering why Master did not make me join the Head Office first, arranged for an induction, and then sent me to other locations. But I guess that is how he worked. He was a different person now. All his care and worries as a friend were lost as we entered this new relation.

I had already signed a five-year bond with him. This bond was in my favour. We were employer and employee now. I got a handsome package, lots of liberty but some strange conditions. According to one of them, I could get married but not leave the country. I did not tell Shashank about this bond. Somewhere I was not clear about his intentions of marrying me. Actually, I was not clear if I wanted to marry him.

Gwalior Office was new and not as big as my old office in Pune This office had a few yet sensible people. They did not waste their time in the canteen. They discussed only work.

I was introduced to two local reporters, who covered politics, crime, social, and public news for region in the four-page special edition. They were instructed to focus on Pahargarh and nearby areas, as there were many wrong doings that were not brought to light.

"Why were they not brought to light?" I asked them, though it was a stupid question, not expected from someone who would soon be heading their division.

Without making me feel embarrassed Gujar Singh replied, "Madam as long as we know we do not have proper evidence, we cannot take chances." He was a short heighted, ugly looking guy, who had a good command on his work. His answer helped me to overcome my inhibitions, because I knew I could ask him anything and he would give me the exact answers.

He seemed like a person on mission and while interacting with him I got to know that he was from Pahargarh and had connections with many local people. There was this new public column "Exposing Sach" for which they had been given a target of 100 stories for that year, if their stories were good enough to get coverage in the main edition and if they receive a good response from readers, then team Gwalior was to get an incentive of two lakh Rupees. The objective was not about exposing any individual, but bringing to light the struggle of a common man.

I went through the list of stories they had gathered. These stories were of people who never got support from police and were forced to take the route of crime for justice. They could have been stories in technical terms but on human grounds they touched my heart. I felt like fighting for their justice.

I was amazed at the work Gwalior team had done risking their life and felt fortunate to have got the opportunity to work with such brave men. Their task could have taken them close to death, but the incentive of two lakh, was enough to keep their motivation to live long, high. Gujar Singh taught me a lot and I am thankful to him to the core.

On one of the usual days when Gujar Singh and team were in action, I joined them for the adventure. After the mission we were sitting in a *dhaba* on the highway. As soon as our *chai* came, a jeep with three policemen along with a prisoner stopped in front of us.

Of all the people I looked at the prisoner. It was for the first time I saw such a scene. He was tall, wore black shirt and denim jeans. He had broad chest, untidy brown hair, big lips but deep eyes. His eyes caught my attention. His hands were tied. On looking at the tired *hawaldaars* it was clear that getting hold of him must have been a task for them. He looked so hot to me.

In a few seconds we saw the *dhaba* on fire and I found myself in the police jeep with the culprit. He was taking me away from my group, far and far away in the dark. But I did not shout, nor did I ask him to leave my hand. He thought I would jump off the moving jeep.

"I am not going to jump," I said. He gave me a sexy look and let go of my hand. I regretted those words.

He stopped the jeep in a strange dark place. It was more like a jungle, and now I was really scared. 'He is a criminal', I said to myself when he gave me that look again.

To my surprise he said, "Yes, I am" in fluent English. After sometime I realized that even he was uncomfortable with me, but for him, leaving me would mean inviting death. Somewhere even I did not want to go.

"What did you do?"

"I killed."

"Killed whom?"

"The rapist."

"Are you mad?"

"Yes, he raped my sister."

"How can someone kill?"

"How can someone rape? Do you want to know how it feels?" two questions from him and I realized that I was standing just in front of my fear. Face to face.

"No, no, please stop it," I said and looked for a place to hide.

He did not say anything. I could stop him with just one 'No'. My fear vanished. It was hard to believe that he was a criminal.

We did not speak the whole night, but I did not sleep the whole night either. He kept his eyes glued on to me for eight hours and so did I.

In the morning I did not know what else to say. Silence was killing me and I could not stop myself from asking him, "Have you fallen in love with me in these eight hours?

"Finally, I saw him blink his eyes, and he gave me a way to leave. But I did not want to go. I stood still.

Looking at me he said, "Okay then I will go."

"But how can I see you again?" I shouted as he was leaving.

"I will know when you are here next, will take you along with me and answer your questions," he said and ran into the jungle. He was a Dacoit who stole my heart. I did not even know his name, and he promised to meet me again. He was sure that I would come back to meet him, and I promised myself that I would.

Soon 'Team Sach' and police were there; I informed them that he left me last night itself, I pretended shocked and disturbed by the whole incident, when actually I had enjoyed it to the core.

My next destination was Jabalpur, which had more news content from the High Court cases and stories of people becoming rich due to increased land rates. It was surprising to see land rates increase, even during recession.

The incentives here were for the salespeople, rather than the journalists. I found it strange, but it was Master Mind's setup. My job was to first understand the world around me and then get into the details.

Then it was Indore on my Agenda and finally after three months I landed in Bhopal, the Head Quarter of 'Sach'. The place did not have enough action. I felt like travelling back to Gwalior.

Meeting with Master was crazy, his way of working was good, but I did not like it. He played memory games with me, and on every point missed I was made to pay a thousand bucks. In the game I lost almost ten grands, but he gained none.

After spending a good amount of time in Bhopal office, I was scheduled to go to Mumbai for six months training in print journalism with Shirish Sir. I was asked not to talk about my connections with 'Sach'. This clause was mentioned in my five years bond.

As the *Rahus* and the *Ketus* of the world played with me, even I tried my luck by challenging them out rightly.

I was excited to meet Neelu after a long time. She had already joined a PR agency and was now staying there independently in a studio apartment close to her office.

After having stayed in the dacoit area for almost one month and having seen murders, kidnaps and other crime, so closely, Mumbai was not a big deal for me. Even my office was in South Mumbai, so I decided to stay with her for six months.

The initial training days were tough. Shirish Sir was very strict and extremely short-tempered. Communication with him needed to be straight to the point; he never liked the Bhopali *'Bataule Baji'*. He showed me a new shade of his *'Rudra Avatar'* at every mistake that I made. For me, getting over that dacoit, from Chambal, was not easy. It was as if I *was* possessed.

At *'The Times of Hindustan'*, sun never used to set. The excitement was on 24x7. On one side I was working with the print journalists, and on the other side I was a part of Shirish Sir's weekly show's core team. I could hardly go home on time. Many times, Neelu used to get irritated with me.

He was a terror and a man with no mercy for anyone. His philosophy was very simple, 'Just fire the bastard if he does not perform.' He could do anything to get the best result from his people and would not mind stooping down, to any level, to get maximum TRPs for his show.

He was full of himself and arrogant to the core. I used to wonder what he saw in Master to agree to mentor 'Sach'.

There were strange stories about his arrogance, circulating in office. He would never let anyone sit next to him, but he knew how to get the best performance out of his team, which is what he was respected for.

Many people, who worked under him, have become big shots in the industry. He had given shape to careers of many. He was still single and it was obvious, no decent girl would agree to marry him.

I used to take his scolding sportingly because just like others, even I knew there could be nothing bigger than getting a chance to work with him.'

*****

Chapter 12

Will Never Let You Down

Be it in the middle of the sea or sand

Darling will never leave your hand

Will build a castle on our dreamland

Together we will live a life grand.

"Gresh, where are you lost?" said Neelakshi, getting her back from the old days.

"Nothing Neelu, tell me."

"Dabbu is not picking up anyone's phone, please check the status."

"I called him Neelu, but he messaged back saying that he was busy. There is a lot of pressure from everywhere. He would call when free."

"Ok, we are all in my room; you can join us once you are done Gresh."

"Sure, Neelu."

Everyone met after lunch. There was a strange tension after Rajat received a message on his cell phone. It said that 'I warned him before had but he did not listen. Look what happened.'

"Guys, I am sure this is meant for Keval. I received a message from the same number just after my wife's death. We need to trace this number–9342345675," said Rajat.

"Just repeat the number Shady," said Neelakshi.

"9342345675"

"How can this be possible?"

"Meaning?"

"I mean Shady, this is Keval's Pune number. Do you remember, we both had the same number except for the last two digits?"

"What, who has this number now?"

"I have no clue."

The tension remained as Maa Sahab entered and declared that she was planning to join politics. They did not know what to say. As it is, neither were they directly involved with 'Sach Party', nor were sure of its fate.

She might have taken this decision under somebody's influence, but she was not aware of the gravity of the situation. Just six friends could not take her to the level that her son was. It needed a cruel heart along with a sharp mind, which the mother of the dead son did not have.

Everyone remained quiet, and Maa Sahab left the room without saying anything more. Greshma followed her to make her feel comfortable. Neelakshi saw her go and felt good about her gesture. She thought about the time when Neelakshi moved to Mumbai,

*****

'After Greshma left for the new job, it was not possible for her to come to Pune. So even I accepted Master's idea of shifting to a PR firm and pursue my career in that field. I got into the best firm of Mumbai. Shifting to Mumbai was not difficult.

The basic model of this industry was to cover the dark and bring the brighter aspect to light, be it, person's image, product's image, company's image, or an association's image. This industry practically enhances the public image, and I was strong at doing that. So, I entered this world without any hassles.

I was sick of staying alone, and my father was not happy with my decision of moving to Mumbai. He never liked the industry that I was getting into. For outsiders it did not hold a good reputation. He was upset and concerned about my future. Many times, my father would curse Gresh for being selfish and leaving me alone.

My first client was from a Health Care and Well-Being industry which was into manufacturing condom. They had come up with a new range, so the first step was to get product exposure for them in good magazines.

There was a debate between the client and its creative agency on defining the Target Group from PR point of view. Since the ad was cleverly made showing a "happy woman for the man who makes a clever choice." Creative agency suggested males, but from the PR aspect we believed that it had a wider audience base.

Finally, it was decided that the exposure, the product story, the brand story, the health story, and the pleasure story would be carried in both male and female centric magazines and the size of articles will keep increasing with every exposure. We agreed to minimum 6 exposures in a month, along with free entry in health camps and product sampling. We chose two media vehicles - magazines and internet.

Product Sampling was something very new to me. How can condoms be sampled, through a magazine or online request. That would be so cheap. But somehow, I had to convince the client because that is where magazines would make money; otherwise they were not ready to carry articles.

It was for the first time I ever saw a condom. Made of rubber, it promised safe sex and no babies.'

*****

She got goose bumps as she thought having touched them, the very first time. Keval Kishore had come to Mumbai during that time.

*****

"What are you saying baby, you have never seen a condom?" he asked surprised.

"No stupid, it's so funny, I just threw as I touched, and weird feeling it gave me,"

"Hmm ok so you have not grown to that level of understanding, till even now. It's my mistake to have kept you away from this information. You are still stuck at base 2 with me. I was too busy with work baby."

"Keval, are you mad? What the hell are you talking? What base 2 crap are you giving me?" I shouted at him, not ready to accept that, after all he was a man.

And suddenly, saw him coming out from the bathroom all naked.

That was a sign of danger, he held me with his strong, really strong arms, I could not escape. He loved me his usual way and then that love moved to levels above base 2. Finally, I had my first sexual experience with him and he was wearing the same condom.

To me everything looked so still, I thought I had lost something, but at the same time I thought I had gained a lot more.

From then on whenever Master would come to Mumbai, he would stay with me.'

*****

Neelakshi thought of the time when Greshma moved in with her in Mumbai, during her training with *The Times of Hindustan*. Whenever Keval would come, she would make an onsite work excuse, and stay with him in his hotel as "Mrs Rajput". Her work was going well; she was learning a lot of things and was quick. "Quick" is the word in this industry for smart people. They know how to get their jobs done.

*****

Papa started pursuing me to get married, and when Gresh was there, they thought it was an opportunity to make both of us go together and meet the prospects. We used to happily go, eat home-made food, made by could be mother-in-laws; leave a good impression on them and crib after coming home.

If by chance the guy was not staying with his family, then Gresh would make sure that she flirted so much with him that he got irritated. Gresh was not really happy doing this. She sometimes would say that she wanted me to get married.' Neelakshi fell asleep after sometime.

*****

Greshma finally got connected to Karan over the phone, "Where are you Dabbu?"

"Hey Gresh, I am tied up in marathon meetings, there is a lot of chaos here, I can't even tell you, what all is going on. These politicians are crazy and I am pursuing them to support the party in the same way, as I used to pursue God before we discovered paper stealing route to pass the exams."

"Was this a joke, Dabbu?"

"No Gresh, you don't understand. You can be confident only on two grounds either when you have the knowledge or you are totally unaware of the consequences. When you are in the middle of these extremes, you are helpless."

"Just like how we were with Master Mind."

"Gresh that was past, please look ahead and try to understand the situation."

"I understand, Dabbu. Anyway, everyone has been trying to reach you. We are all at Rajput's *Haveli* wondering about what should be the next step."

"Don't tell me everyone's together, after so many years. Have you all started the dissection of old chapters?"

"What chapters dude?"

"Gresh, I am not talking to a dumb village woman. You know what I am talking about."

"No man and I don't want to get into it; we all have our dirty secrets and opening up the old chapters would be like opening a Pandora's Box."

"Ok Gresh let's not get into it, as of here I am working on something big so please tell everyone not to worry."

"I know Dabbu you would get us out of this mess."

"I am trying to, Gresh. Do you remember all crimes that we did in the dark; have I ever let you down? Only I know the secret of your stupid honest eyes, when even your husband suspects you of sleeping with me. He would never understand our friendship."

"I am sure you will be able to handle it. But if you need your partner in crime, just let me know. I don't care what people think."

"Please tell your husband, that your friend will not let his investors suffer, ask him to have some patience. I am sure the fact that I picked your phone and not his would irritate him even more, but am really tied up."

"Relax, dude. Bye and take care," said Greshma as Shashank entered the room.

"I am sorry, Gresh, for hurting you. I know had it not been this tragedy you would have not spoken to me. It's already more than a year since we spent time together, after the Ladakh trip," said Shashank.

"Shashank please I don't want to talk about the past. Let's just keep it the way it is. For me work is important and after giving so much to my career you can't expect me to sit at home. I am not an uneducated mother. I am able to handle Hridaan even alone." Tears were ready to roll down her cheeks.

"I am sorry Gresh, I was concerned about your health and yes somewhere was getting over possessive." He said and held her in his arms, kissed on her forehead, "I missed you a lot Gresh." Listening to him, she started to cry.

"Do you even know, Shashank, how much I fought with myself to be with you?"

She paused, wiped her tears and continued; "Remember when I was in the last days of my first training in Mumbai, Papa had come for his friend's daughter's wedding. I went along with Neelu to meet him."

"Yes, I remember, you had mentioned to me before going, but never said anything about what happened after the meeting."

"I did not want to go alone, as I thought he had invited some prospective family to meet me and approve me for my good nature and looks. The whole world had already given me a character certificate for all the obvious reasons."

"How can you be so pathetic, Gresh?"

"What Pathetic Shashank don't you know how our society is? I made sure I looked bad, I wore my old shirt, fade jeans and messed up my hair. It was not possible for me to talk badly in front of my father, so that was my way to rebel; I hated the idea of being showcased."

"Oh Gresh, how can you even think you would look bad. You are mad." Bank said and kissed her on lips.

"Shut up, will you?" she snapped, releasing herself and demanded a decent behaviour.

"Ok then what happened?"

She went on; "As we knocked the door, our heartbeat was really fast and when we saw Papa at the door in full formals, it was clear that something was wrong. I kept wondering if the people inside were arrogant Rajputs. We went in, but to my surprise there was no one. It was a little relief for me, but then I thought we are early."

"Then did they come?"

"No, Papa had something else in mind. He looked at Neelu and said that both of us have been given enough time to build our career and we should now get serious about marriage."

"Then?"

"Then you won't believe what happened, suddenly he said in his typical Rewa tone, *Kaheen koi Bangali to pakad kar hamare samne nahi laa dogi na.*"

Shashank took his hands off Greshma's and screamed, "You never told me about this clause Gresh, do you even know what I had to face in your house?"

"What clause?"

"Being a Bengali clause, your father was all set to kill me."

"Please don't over react Shashank. He did nothing."

"I am alive only because of your mother, who let me take charge, after he got a heart attack. You did whatever you felt comfortable with, and I had to face the brunt of it. That visit to India was strange."

"I wish you had not come, Shashank," she said and started crying, as if there was some deep pain hidden inside; "I could never forgive Master."

"Gresh please control yourself, Master is no more with us and for me it is you who is important in which every way."

His mobile phone started to ring, and he went to receive it.

Chapter 13

The Black and the White

Nothing is black, nothing is white

The world is full of wrong and right

You lose if for you hold on to rules tight

In this game right is wrong, even wrong is right

"Yes, I am coming to US next week. Everything will be fine this week. Just tell the investors not to worry," said Shashank over phone and went out to meet Raj.

Greshma quietly watched him go. She could not get over that night when she went to Delhi to receive Shashank. He had come only to meet her parents almost three years after he left.

After her training with *The Times of Hindustan,* she was back and went to Gwalior office of 'Sach'. Lot of crime stories were spilling out and there was a huge movement started by the local people against tolerance.

Keval wanted to accompany her and they decided to go by road, so that she could finish her work on the way. It was for the first time she was travelling with him. She was on cloud nine, as she was to meet Shashank after a long time. There was no limit to the speed at which they drove.

She was very happy with the way her life had progressed. The flight was very early in the morning, so they decided to reach Delhi in the evening. In one year's, time she had almost forgotten about the man with honest eyes.

She went back to that drive to Delhi.

*****

'The journey was tiring, but we chatted a lot. Master spoke at length; there were funny jokes about college, fun that boys had together, in fact there were so many interesting things I did not know about Shashank.

Master Mind met him four times in the US, on his business trips. He had a lot to tell about those visits, and how people there feel lonely when they are away from family and friends in a different country, how difficult life becomes, how freely available sex was, about why men went to Bangkok, about how men betray their partners and a lot more."

I kept on listening to whatever he said quietly. Infidelity was something I never thought of, from a man who was struggling so hard, only for me.

Master went on and on and on...and soon the journey was over. We came to the hotel, which very close to the airport.

I was sitting in the room thinking about the new doubts that Keval had planted in my mind. It was late, I was just out after the shower in my bath robe and I heard the bell.

"Who is this?"

"Open the door girl it's me," said the voice and that was Master.

"Master, will you wait for two minutes?"

"Please Gresh need to use your washroom, I forgot my room key inside."

Not knowing what to do, I waited for a while and let him into the washroom. He rushed in and puked.

"Oh God, what was that Master? You are not well? Or is it food poisoning?"

"*Kal ki utri nahi yaar,* and this journey plus no lunch break messed it all. Sorry, it was so urgent that I did not have the time to call for service."

"Have water and you will feel better. But when did you get the time to drink yesterday?"

"Please Gresh don't behave like Neelu, there is no need to find a *Mahurat* to drink? Can I please have a quick shower in your bathroom and we will go down to eat?"

"Ok dude, but come fast and please clean the mess."

I was all set to go into the washroom as soon as he was out, ignoring his presence, I quickly wanted to get going and get into my clothes. As he came out in the towel, I felt a little conscious.

"Just one minute," he said and stopped me at the door as I tried to avoid any eye contact; he went inside, apparently touching me with his sides, got his clothes out and again said, "Just one more minute, Gresh."

"What, just say fast I need to go in?" I said in an unwelcoming hesitant tone.

"Do you remember the list of boys who loved you in college?"

"Yes, idiot, I remember. Let me come back and we will talk about it," I said, putting a fake smile on my face and making an effort to hide my fear of getting raped. Except for Neelu, nobody was aware of that fear.

He came to me and kept my clothes on the table, "Good. Gresh do you remember I told you I was upset last year because of a friend who was cheating on his girlfriend?"

"Yes, idiot, I do remember and you said you were good friends with the couple. I am going now."

He was just not letting me go, "Good, do you want to know who that was?"

"No, idiot, I don't want to know. Let me get ready you are not in your senses," I said, jerking his hand and trying to leave from that corner.

"You will go mad if I tell you the name."

"As if you would say Shashank and I would believe you. Keval please leave."

"Yes, it is Shashank," he said straight, looking into my eyes.

"No Keval, it can't be him; he can't deceive me. He knows I will kill him."

"I am sorry Gresh, but yes this is true," he said lowering his voice making it more believable and authentic.

It was hard to believe, but yes, it was not impossible too. Shashank had mentioned once, when I was not giving him enough time that he felt lonely. He even warned me that if I continued, he would find someone else. I never thought he would.

Keval was making me believe him. It was as if I had lost the ground beneath me. It was blackout for a second. Keval held me tight as if to console me. It was so tight that he could feel my inches from the still wet cotton cloth that covered me.

He was not a friend at that time nor was he my employer. He was just another man, "Do you know Gresh in the list of boys, I was the first one to have wanted to approach you, but I never had the courage to come up to you. You are so beautiful, that I was just mesmerized by your charm."

It was the biggest shock of my life, "Are you mad? Why are you men like this?" I gave him a jerk to let me free. I was broken by Shashank's infidelity and somewhere I wanted to take revenge. Master was already on his peak of emotional conviction and I wanted to believe him; "I am sorry Gresh, truth just slipped out, I did not want to tell you. It disturbed me and now it is disturbing you," he said and kissed me tight. He did not let me out of his grip despite my efforts.

I started searching for honesty in his eyes; I neither reacted to his touch nor jerked him back.

"I hate Shashank and want to punish him and punish him to death. I will slap him when he comes. Keval just be by my side," I said, and he brought me closer to him. The fear in me was dead.

"How would your slap make a difference to his life, he will beg you to forgive and if you don't, at the most he would get married to someone else and settle in the US. You will be the one to suffer. You have to give him back in the same coin."

"How will I do that, Keval?"

Throwing his trap of words at her he said, "Do you remember Gresh; you said you would repay my help."

"Yes, I am a Rajput; we don't keep anybody's favour."

"So just promise me that you will forget everything once we step out of this room tomorrow morning," he said.

"Tomorrow morning means what Keval?"

"You want to take revenge from him, right?" he asked firmly, looking into my eyes to hear a yes and continued; "This revenge must be in the same coin '*Dhokha*' right?" this was an even more affirmative tone and I could not say anything but, 'yes', I again looked into his eyes but there was no love for me, it was only lust.

"Can I remove your bathrobe?" He asked.

"What?"

"Only if you say yes, Gresh we are always friends and it will never affect our relation and you have promised me you will forget it once we are out. I will never ever talk about it in my life. But you should never let the criminal go. How else do you think can you do equal justice to what he has done?" he continued trying to convince me.

Taking charge of self, I took a deep breath, shook Master off my body and said "yes you can."

Then happened what should have never happened. There was no dinner that night only, the three letter act wild and loud which went on and on, till next morning. We got back to self before Shashank arrived and as promised, never spoke about it ever and continued to work the same way as we, guilty of practically nothing.

I could never confront Shashank, but could not keep it to myself either. I wrote to him in a letter, he neither apologized to me nor accused me for anything. As if he seconded Keval's words, 'Promise me that you will forget everything once we are out of this room next morning.'

How can these men just use women, for the satisfaction of their inflated ego? I hate Master for making me walk this dirty path. **And that is the reason why I wanted to kill him.'**

*****

As Shashank came back to Gresh and saw her eyes and nose red after crying, he ran up to her. For him it was the last thing in the world he could see; her tears. Now that Keval was dead there was practically no one to fight against, but he had to get his Gresh back. Back from the web that Keval had weaved around them. Shashank went back to the time,

*****

I wanted to take Greshma back to the US after marriage, but somewhere Keval had got her to sign some five-year bond about which Greshma never spoke until our marriage. Keval, on the other hand, showed me a carrot of Economic boom in India, which created a lot of opportunities for Foreign Investors. There was another agreement that he signed with me under which I was supposed to get Foreign Investors for his projects in exchange of crores of Dollars once my target was complete. It was not an easy target, but real men accept challenge without fear. I slogged to the level that my plan to settle in the US seemed failing, and I kept on shuttling between the two countries. My relation with Greshma went through a lot of ups and downs during the process.

There was no point in telling or blaming her for anything, because even I was caught in the same web. All I could do was, just get married to her, so that she was secured and I was relieved that no one would harm her whether I am in India or abroad. Hoping that we would be relieved of the trap one day, I parallelly started working on the plan of having my own investment firm.

Since the market outside was not good, people had no money to invest. India showed growth and I decided to find investors within India. The only objective was to complete the target.

I was in problems from all sides and yet alone. It was a battle that I was fighting with my own self. A new mental challenge waited for me every first day of the week when I had to meet Keval. The meeting ended in humiliation most of the time. I felt trapped, my life was controlled by someone whose finances were in my control, once upon a time and *that is why I wanted to kill Keval.'*

He goes to Greshma and wipes her tears.

*****

"My red pumpkin, do you even know how I convinced your adamant Rajput father for our marriage?"

"Yes, a bit of it. I was in Gwalior for work at that time. I just told him that there is a guy who is coming to meet."

"Exactly as you did not tell them anything about me, and that is what created problem for me. When I entered the house all your relatives were there. The first sight of your house was scary, and the danger increased as time passed by."

"What rubbish, I am sure; *chotu* must have offered you his chocolate. He is a very sweet kid. He is my favourite nephew."

"Yes, actually, he was the one who made me comfortable. As I entered, heard a woman saying, *ladka to puraa round hai, bass Bangali na ho*, and I was shocked to hear that."

"I am sure that must be *choti chaachi*, she loves to make a fuss about things."

"May be and then there was a list of questions which started with your father and could have ended with my life."

"What question-and-answer session did you have?"

"Our society is said to be male dominating but, it's only when you enter an Indian family do you realize the importance of it. The head of the family is responsible for every individual under his shelter, and your father loves you a lot Gresh. I don't know if I remember all the questions, but still would try it for you

Question 1 – so you are from US?

Answer 1 - Uncle, I have completed my MS from there and now am working in the US.

Question 2 – how do you know Greshma?

Answer 2 – we used to study in the same college.

Question 3 – were you having an affair?

Answer 3 – No.

Question 4 – Why do you want to marry her?

Answer 4 – I liked her and when I proposed to her, on the last day of college she said she would not marry against her family's wish. When I am on my feet, I could ask for her hand.

Question 5 – What does your father do?

Answer 5 – He works with a government bank. There are four years for him to retire.

Question 6 – Who else is there in your family?

Answer 6 – My mother is a house wife and elder sister is married in Australia. She just had a baby girl and everybody has gone to see her.

Question 7 – Where do you belong to?

Answer 7 - Papa is from Bilaspur and Mummy is from Raipur.

Question 8 – Are you going to stay in the US itself?

Answer 8 – Yes Uncle, it has good growth opportunities.

Question 9 – Do you know Greshma wants to work?

Answer 9 – Yes uncle, we will work that out.

Question 10 – Are your parents fine with this marriage?

Answer 10 – They are fine with my choice.

Question 11 – Till when can you marry?

Answer 11 – Today itself, if you agree.

Question 12 – But we won't confirm unless we meet your parents.

Answer 12 – Uncle next month they are coming along with didi.

Question 13 –What is your name you said?

Answer 13 – Ji Shashank (I coughed) Sharma.

Question 14 – So you are not a Bengali, but a Brahmin right.

Answer 14 – I was shocked to death, but finally managed to tell them the truth. After that your father got an ancestral gun. A huge drama was created and suddenly we realized that he had a heart stroke. We rushed him to the hospital, but his doctor was on leave. I immediately asked my friend's father who is also a doctor to help us out and thankfully all was well. Your mother supported me a lot. Your brothers were against my interference, but she let me proceed. Finally, Gresh after three months, I got an approval for our marriage, when you did not even care."

"I am sorry Shashank for putting you through so much."

"I love you Gresh, and that's your style for which I like you. I have been a little possessive of you, but at the same time there were some issues which I could not discuss with you. I was equally trapped as you were. I am sorry too."

Finally, Greshma smiled, and it was time for everyone to collect in the hall for evening tea.

Chapter 14

The U Turn

To succeed, the road is not straight

Hard work is the key to become great

Success road has exciting twists and turns

The journey would give many heart burns

Pahargarh never saw the entire 'Scorpio Group' together; it was for the first time that five of them were under the 200 years old roof of Rajput Haveli, yet it felt like they were a part of it. This land had bound all of them together for some unknown reason. Just as their birth was a mystery for them, so was their reason to be together. They thought it was friendship for a very long time.

They were still unaware of the basic reason that drew them all to Pahargarh when practically they had nothing to do there. Not that they were still unaware of the true colours of the dead men, but still they pretended to be ignorant about all they had been through.

"There is an interesting line in this article on Keval," said Raj.

"What is it?" asked Rajat.

"A series of co-incidents made him the Hero."

"What are they?" asked Greshma.

"It is not mentioned clearly."

"They are not aware that there is a lot more involved in the making of their Hero," said Greshma curtly.

"They say he was not on good terms with his father, who died after his son's death," said Raj.

"Media will talk all sorts of things, they would not mind digging into the neighbour's grave to get publicity, even if the facts are irrelevant. That's their job; don't get carried away by their lack of factual knowledge. Worst part is, despite having all the power, Media is the last one to know the truth. And I proudly represent my profession," said Greshma.

The Industrial Zone project had its own important place for everyone. They all played an important role in the execution of the same. It helped them earn and make a mark in their career.

"I did not come here after the launch. Only I know the tussle I faced in getting the approvals," said Raj.

"Why tussle, I heard that everything was within the norms?" asked Rajat.

"No man, this was one of the biggest Industrial belts of the country, and since there were plans to improve the road connectivity across the country, we decided to jack the land rates. And we hired E&Z business consultants to make a pitch presentation for clients. This showed the future benefits and cost savings which the industries would have, in the long run. These rates were much higher than the market rate," said Raj.

"I got foreign investors to put their industries there, but and the rates were really high," said Shashank.

"I know getting approval on those rates was also not easy dude, and another big tension was pharma industry. Their association was putting political pressure on us to reduce rates" said Raj.

"Then what did you all do?" asked Greshma.

"Nothing we had to play safe, there was a pocket created only for pharma with reduced rates on immediate booking," said Raj.

"Did this trick work?" asked Neelakshi.

"Only I know how I managed it, after all the project promised a lot of money," replied Raj with a strange smile.

Greshma was away during the time of development of the Industrial Zone project.

After being betrayed by the two men who were close to her heart, she was broken and did not know where to go. All she could see was the road to Chambal. She went there in search of the dacoit who stole her heart. Neither did she inform anyone, nor did anyone ask her. They had no right to ask her.

Ramu Kaka came to call them, as the car was ready to take them to the Industrial Zone. It was at a distance of one-hour drive from Pahargarh. All the men went there, while women preferred to stay back.

After the men left, Greshma connected back with the old time.

*****

'Within a minute of my stepping down at the bus stand, a child came to me. He knew I had come to get my answers. I followed that child blindly without even realizing where he was taking me. It was a dark jungle that I was passing through, scary one. A person could easily get lost with no trace, in that maze. I was getting absorbed into them so much so that I lost my mind and there stood the man whose eyes drew me back.

The child went and I was all alone with the man. I asked him, "Will you ever leave me alone?"

"Only if I die."

"Will you love me till death?"

"I don't want to die," he replied and I knew he wanted to be with me for all his life.

When I allowed his honest eyes to touch me, I did not feel dirty; I loved the touch of those eyes, hands and his body. It seemed like I was pure now, after the dirty touch of Master Mind.

I was out of that shock, as I had discovered true love. I was with him for more than fifteen days, till a bullet came from somewhere and took his life. He died in my arms and I was the reason for his death. I made him weak, and the people from his clan did not want to see him alive anymore.

He died naked, and I struggled to cover myself as I ran away from those honest eyes. That was the last time I saw them and knew would never be able to see them again.

I buried all my emotions with his death, became strong, and went back to fight the world of cruel men.

In those fifteen days Neelakshi and Keval met the MLA of Pahargarh, Shivam Raj Singh, who incidentally was also friends with the Rajputs for generations. He had a soft corner for Keval's father who helped him in his tough times but as a good politician did not offer any direct help, as a friend in need he guided Keval to the right path.'

*****

Looking at Greshma lost in her thoughts, Neelakshi called her, "Gresh do you know about the meeting with Shivam Raj Singh, which I attended with Keval. That was my first visit to Pahargarh?"

"Yes Neels, I could not make it then, in fact you had once mentioned that the red *kurta* I gave you, had started proving lucky for you," said Greshma and went towards her room.

Neelakshi smiled at Greshma as she went, switched on the light of the living room and thought about that meeting,

*****

Yes, my lucky red *kurta*, after that I always wore it for my important meetings. Master's father was totally against taking any kind of political help from MLA Shivam Raj Singh, but Master had decided that he would.

He took an appointment of early in the morning and before the clock could strike 8:30; we were at the main gate of Singh's *Haveli*. As we entered, we passed through a big lawn with a green carpet of grass. Rose beds of various colours covered the left side of the lawn.

Unlike all ancient *havelis*, the front elevation of *Singh Haveli* was different; it was not made of Red Stone, but had a lovely glass design from all sides. They say a German architect had designed it some 86 years back. In Pahargarh *Singh's Haveli* was famous as '*Sheesh Mahal*'. People used to love receiving invitation from *Singh Haveli*.

As we entered the *haveli*, we were taken to the *Baithak* (drawing room). It was a big hall with white walls on three sides and white curtains on the fourth side. The front side had French windows and the entrance door from where we came in, was to the left side of the front wall. They believed that there should to be only one door in the house, as *Maa Lakshmi* entered from there, a second door indicates her exit so they did not have another door in the huge *Haveli*.

We were asked to wait for two minutes, as he was performing his morning *pooja*. They were said to be descendents of Lord Surya and so morning and evening pooja was a daily ritual.

As we waited for him, we tried to understand the mindset of people of the *Haveli, looking at* the interior. The three walls were decorated with heads of dead wild animals - Tiger, Deer, Cheeta and many more. I was sure they must have been killed during the famous '*Rajput Shikaar*' which was one of their main sources of recreation. It was the symbol of their fake '*Rajput Shaan*' till the government became strict, and imposed a ban on killing animals.

Without wasting much time, Shivam Singh joined us. Keval stood up, touched his feet, *"Pranaam Tauji."*

"Khush Raho Rajput, Bhai Sahab kaise hain?"

"Ji apka ashirwaad hai tauji. Sab achha hai. Taiji aur Sheetal nazaar nahi aa rahe hain?"

"Haan beta wo apni mama ke ghar gai hain."

There was a little family discussion on their *pushtaini* fights and Pahargarh life for some time, till Shivam Raj Singh noticed me, a girl with Keval Kishore Rajput. *"Beta Aapki Taarif."*

"Tauji she is my colleague, she is helping me in the project that I was talking to you about," said Keval.

I did not like the way Keval introduced me, I was not just helping him. I was his past, his present, and his future. Why did he not introduce me as his life partner? I felt like beheading him and decorating empty place next to the tiger's head on the wall. But I smiled, as my new job with India's top PR agency had taught me professionalism.

"Oh yes, tell me about that project, *Beta.* Where do you need my help?"

"Tauji, I want to build cement factory on Dadaji's land that is next to yours in Tretra, next to Pahargarh."

"You mean the same land which is under dispute since your grandfather's time?"

"Ji; Chaachaji has encroached it; and it's a huge land. I can easily get sanction for mines, close to that place, since my friend Dabbu's uncle is heading the mining department and we can have a new plant, bigger than the ones in Satna.

If you agree, then we can combine your land as well, and work on getting approval for setting up a complete Industrial Zone. Selling that land will be my responsibility," said Keval as I looked at him with my eyes wide open. It meant a lot of work for my PR agency, as I would have to create good-will for that land.

The project had a huge potential and was big enough for me to form my own PR agency and I decided at that very moment, I will.

In just three and a half years of work experience, I was capable of setting up my own company. Just the thought gave me a high.

Shivam Raj Singh looked very impressed, "Keval Beta, I will give you a *wazir* to play a game against them and by no chance will you lose. Once you get your land we will work on your project."

"But why don't you directly help me *Tauji*?"

"Beta, your father taught you to dare and enter the game, but how to play it, is what this politician *Tauji* would teach you. Once you win, you will get the answer."

"Who is that *Wazir, Tauji*?"

"*Baghi* Mangal Singh."

"What? A Dacoit! You mean a *daku* will help me get my land back. This is not a small *chori chakari Tauji*, it's a land."

"I know Beta, and there is a very old story behind this particular family connection. Trust me, your *chaachaji* will not only give the land papers back, but he will also never dare to interfere in your work."

"What story is this *Tauji*?"

"You don't have to get into this. If you trust your *tauji*, just do as I say."

"How can I meet him?"

"You will find him in *Chambal Ghati*, the ravines which are homes to many *Baghi*s."

"How will I find him there? Can you give me his mobile number?

"He smiled at these questions and said, "Don't worry, they will find you.""

I became really excited with the whole *daku* connection, and without even thinking about the seriousness of the conversation, just intervened, "You mean *Tauji*, these people still exist?"

"Yes, they exist and are a part of the society as much as we are. Their existence disciplines many people in society whom we can't," replied Shivam Singh and asked us to go to the bus stand close to Chambal after a week. Mangal Singh's men would take us to him and he will hand over the papers to us.

I was amazed at this system that worked with such a precision. Like idiots, we slog for targets, identifying goals and achieve nothing. I felt like saluting these people. They remind me of *ballu bhaiya*.

The work was done in one week's time, as promised by Shivam Raj Singh. We got to know that Keval's great grandfather received this piece of land for his contribution in the development of Nagpur Gondia railway track during the British era.

Along with a fertile land, on Indore Dewas highway, they also gave him this land parcel, which was close to his native place. His grandfather whose name was also 'Keval Kishore Rajput' had kept those papers safely with him. During his last days, he shifted to Pahargarh. It was then that Keval's cousins caught hold of those papers and encroached on the land.

Daku Mangal Singh's story was also strange, Keval's cousin uncle had raped his sister, and she tried to commit suicide. Mangal Singh, who was not a dacoit then, killed Keval's cousin uncle's elder brother and when he was about to kill his uncle, his great grandfather said that he would accept his sister as his daughter-in-law and got him married to his uncle.

And that was the reason his father was not in favour of Master getting close to Shivam Raj Singh. It exposed dark secrets that were buried since ages. The ravines of Chambal are full of mysterious stories.

Once the land papers were in hand, it was the cement plant in mind and a lot of approvals. Shark started his work of getting approval for the Industrial Zone as well; he was promised big money on getting that sanction. Shivam Raj Singh agreed for the Joint Venture.

I started on my work of understanding the markets and media, which would fetch us quicker results to attract buyers of land. After one year I was to launch my own PR agency with Rajput as my first client. Dabbu's uncle approved the mining proposal and his commission was fixed in it. Everything seemed so happening, but back in the Rajput Mansion, there were two Rajputs who were not in conversation terms, with each other. There were reasons for it but it was known only to them.

The project took almost two years. We celebrated our 29th birthday week with the launch of this project. After which, Keval and I went on a holiday to Singapore. A month after the trip, realized that I was pregnant.

*****

Chapter 15

Everything has a Reason

If I exist there is a reason

Every smile has a reason

No sorrow comes without a reason

If it moves, then there is a reason

The Little Kishore was back after playing with his new friends. Ramu Kaka brought him a glass of milk and some biscuits. They switched on the television; news channels only spoke about Kishore Keval Rajput. Neelakshi did not want Little Kishore to get affected by it anymore. So, she started flipping channels.

"Hey that is Shady Uncle," she said to Little Kishore as she saw his comedy show 'The Rajat's'.

"I don't miss his show," she said, looking at Greshma.

"I know Neels it's so nice to see him back after a two-year gap. Do you know the first episode of this series got the highest TRPs in the history of Indian television?" said Greshma.

"I know that. I used it for my PR while working on his 'come back' campaign. Thank God he is out of that mess."

"Remember, after we all had left Pune, he decided to leave his job and finally try his luck as a stand-up comedian."

"Yes, I know, and the reason behind it was none other than Keval Kishore Rajput. Man, who showered me with a confused status in his life. The whole world is making fun of me."

"What are you saying Neelu?"

"You think I don't know Gresh, even you have been giving fillers to people."

"Are you mad?"

"I am not Gresh, news that are making rounds on television were once upon a time kept secrets between two friends who understood each other more than anyone else in the world."

"Neelu, I did not tell anything to anyone. Why don't you understand your life had been under scrutiny ever since you exhibited your love for Keval? Have you ever noticed your own behaviour? Please don't blame me for your wrong."

"Gresh, I know you very well."

"Neelu, I don't want to argue with you on anything. I speak the truth and it hurts you, that is the only difference. Let's not fight, please. It will give a wrong impression to Little Kishore. Tell me, how did Keval contribute to Shady's career?"

"He knew his expertise of winning heart. People believe, and like his style of putting things in such a light-hearted way, that nobody gets offended. He always communicated his message right."

"I know Neelu he is such a rare combination."

"Keval wanted him to do something that brought this real side of him to light. Keval encouraged him to move on, as soon as he was through with paying uncle's debt."

"Neelu, now I really feel you were right in saying that we were all dancing to Keval's tune. How did Kiran react to it?"

"Gresh I was in Mumbai when Shady decided to leave Pune, and Kiran was very upset at his decision. Their love story started in the office and she thought it would end in the office itself."

"Do you know their complete love story, Neels?"

"Yes, of course, Gresh. Their story is really cute, unlike any of ours. I guess your philosophy of two eyes with trust and love for each other was meant for them in a true sense. They just hit it right and got along extremely well."

"How did it begin?"

"It started when you had already left Pune."

"Sounds interesting, I guess Shady took that fight between me and Shark on appraisal issue, very seriously and worked on his 'project girlfriend' immediately after that."

"Looks like he did, but I can't say anything. You know how unpredictable men are and just one was enough to make me mad," said Neelakshi.

"Relax girl there are many more to come, you would not even know, tell me how did they begin?"

"I don't like this attitude of yours, Gresh."

"Chill; you tell me what happened next."

"Despite having a good image in his office, somehow Shady was not satisfied with his work. Every three to four months he would change his department, and this was affecting his appraisal every time. His frustration level kept on increasing day by day.

He was seen sitting in the HR department every alternate day with some argument or the other. HR people soon started avoiding him," said Neelakshi.

"What are you saying, Neels? I never thought he was going that crazy. Did he speak about all this to you?"

"Yes Gresh, just as how Dabbu finds comfort, in venting out his frustration to you, Shady used to find that comfort with me and so did I. This relation can't be given a name, but it does exist in the undercurrent, how much ever Shashank or Keval hate it. There is always another man whose presence completes your complete man," said Neelakshi.

"Exactly, that is what I want to tell you, Neelu. You can't sulk for a dead man. I have left no reason to give any explanation to anyone in my life. I care a damn about which man thinks what. If I feel, then I decide on him. Just move on, Neels."

"It's not even four days Gresh, how do you expect me to be so cruel, and how long will you continue doing that Gresh?"

"Till I don't quench my thirst, Neelu; forget me, did he spare you that you want to mourn for him? People will make a whore out of you. Will you become one?"

"Just shut up, Gresh. I don't want to talk to you."

"Forget us; tell me what happened with them."

"It was just after you left from Pune, did Kiran join Shady's office as an HR executive. She was given the charge of Shady's file.

No one gave his history to her, but she was given no other work either. They knew, if she succeeded in handling him, she would pick any task easily. As it is, she had come through reference, so no one was happy with her.

Her KRA (Key Result Area) for first three months was to settle issues of file number 243 which belonged to Mr Rajat Chandani, our Shady dear. If she performed, she would be confirmed, else would be asked to leave."

"Now that is what I call filmy, Neelu."

"Yes. Initially they started with normal talks, then their talks turned into arguments and then heated arguments, so much so that they were asked to leave the floor, take their fights to the discussion room and come back only when the issues were resolved."

"Amazing, then what happened? I guess they fell in love during those fights."

"That's Shady Neelu; everything has to be dramatic in his life."

"I am sure, but what drama?"

"One evening Kiran was sitting till late evening, making Shady's department transfer papers. He went to check and started shouting for no reason. Luckily, Kiran's boss was also there."

"Then what happened?"

"Then he came out, asked Shady to come into his cabin, and gave him a piece of his mind."

"Why? What did he say Neelu?"

"He blasted him first and then informed that they were planning to fire him this month. It was difficult for the company to afford such an expensive and complicated employee. He praised Kiran, and told him that she fought hard to prove that Shady's presence has added value to the system."

"What are you saying?"

"Yes, Gresh with her efforts Shady was considered for an appraisal after a very long time."

"Don't tell me Neelu, Kiran did so much for that idiot."

"Yes, moreover he asked Shady to ask her, for how many days had she been skipping lunch for his work. He took her out for lunch, the next day and then their love story began."

"So sweet, she must have been really upset when Shady moved to Mumbai."

"Ya she was, but then, it was not even six months and he got a break in the talent hunt show. Within next six months he won the competition and rose to fame. And in next few months he bought his house, called uncle aunty to Mumbai and got married to Kiran. He was all set in just two years and we kept wondering about what was happening."

"I know Neelu his marriage was very simple with only us and his family. Even Kiran's sister could not make it, just her parents. I remember how I managed to attend the wedding. But we had great fun. He was the first one to get married; it took all of us almost five years to settle down in our careers."

"It is normal for everyone, Gresh. It's just that we had bigger dreams and hence had taken bigger risks and paid a bigger price."

"Relax Madam; you are just 33 and too young to talk all this. There is a long life ahead, for you to decide, what price you have paid for which dream," said Greshma and tried to cheer up Neelakshi.

It was already 9:00 pm and guys were back after their visit to the Industrial Zone. Dinner was ready by then.

They went to freshen up; Greshma helped Ramu Kaka as he laid the table, and Neelakshi kept herself busy with Little Kishore. Maa Sahab was just about to finish her dinner as she looked at the kid. He was a cute little boy and reminded her of Keval's childhood. He had the same eyes, same chin and same hair as her son had. He threw the same kind of tantrums while eating as her son did, except that Keval used to talk after every spoon, while Little Kishore ran and made his mother run before every spoon.

*****

As there was time for dinner Greshma waited for everyone to come, thinking about how she had disappeared from the scene while the whole Economic Zone project was commencing. Shashank used to coordinate with Master and helped him to get investors from abroad. Neelakshi was busy coordinating with media. Bank and Dabbu were busy with their work while that was the time when Greshma could not get over the pain of losing the man with trust in his eyes.

*****

I moved to Mumbai with *The Times of Hindustan* overruling the clause in the contract and started staying separately as I did not like the way Neelakshi reacted to my plan of shifting with her again.

Shirish Sir was at his usual worse, but I was ready for anything. All I wanted was to reach to a height where no one could touch me. I used to get harassed every day, but I kept on working and improving myself. I did not care about the number of hours I worked.

And yes, I was engaged to Shashank to get my parents out of the tension. I had still not disclosed the 5-year contract to him; it was already two years since I signed it.

It was after six months in Mumbai office that I realized I was extremely good at giving a right perspective to every story that appeared to become the news. Soon I felt that my training period was over and wanted to give my point of view, to every project that I was handling, both in print and electronic media.

I even wanted Shirish Sir to consider my point of view in his talk shows. But he always avoided and turned them down. He always avoided any eye contact with me.

It used to hurt; I still did not give up. My skills were polished to the level that I could even challenge the people who were much more experienced and senior to me. But Shirish would never consider my views even once.

I did not want to be a cut copy paste data provider. I wanted to host a show. It was already three years of experience in journalism, and I was dying to jump into action.

One evening just before the talk show, I exchanged Shirish Sir's papers with mine. The topic was 'Rape Victims' and I knew no one could have a better opinion on that subject than the victim herself.

I always used to wonder how I survived, and moved against the fear that once had absorbed me. I was never raped, but always felt like a victim. He understood what was done with the papers and I knew he would kill me for it. I was ready and ready to bear the brunt. I was not scared of anything, anymore. I waited, it was 11:30 pm and he did not come out of his cabin.

There were reporters from the late-night shift who were on with their job; our office was never out of action. My mind was inside that cabin with the man who was ruthless of all the men whom I know.

He did use my points, because I left him with no other choice for his LIVE SHOW. One thing was sure that he did not agree with any of those points. Everyone knew what I was going through.

None of them asked why I was not going home; the best part could have been to go home and never come back.

They all thought I was fickle-minded, and that is why I used to resign and come back again. And the part of my story which amused them the most was that Shirish Sir still did not mind taking me back. Well, they were actually unaware of the 'Contract'. There was something serious between Shirish Sir and Keval Kishore Rajput that I never bothered to find.

It was at 2:30 am when I received a call from Shirish Sir and he had called me inside his cabin. Everyone was gone by then. The floor was almost empty, so thankfully there was no witness to my insult.

I felt really scared as I said "coming sir". He knew I was waiting for him, or maybe he saw in the CCTV camera. I was sweating even in the AC. Looking at me, Shashank, Keval, Dabbu or the man with the honest eyes would have called me 'sexy', but I knew this man would kill me.

His huge cabin, thankfully, did not have a camera so there would be no proof of my insult. As I entered with my eyes literally drilling the floor, I could hear my heart beat. He asked me to look straight.

As I looked at him, I saw a pair of honest eyes with love for me. I could not take it and fainted. Morning I saw myself on a huge bed which was not mine, only to realize a naked man sleeping next to me. I did not seem to have resented his touch. He woke up and I saw the same love in his eyes, which got me out of senses.

Who says you don't get when you go out to find something with full conviction? Look people, I have found them back.

It's not difficult for a woman to judge the feelings of a man by just looking into his eyes. If there is honest love, then one look is enough. This feeling in itself is far beyond the mere thrill of physical pleasure.

I thought they were lost forever, but somewhere that urge remained and I found him in Shirish Sir. We got absorbed into each other and I was on top of the world.

It was for the first time that Mr Shirish was in love and that too with me. We did not make our relation public. Yes, he kept on insulting me in office, but that was only because he wanted me to improve my work.

After eight months of our secret relationship he said, "Greshma your views as a journalist are very strong but they need a little toning, and that will come with age. You need to prove yourself to let me give you a chance to host the show.

By the way, it's not that I used your points that day, because there was no other option, but only because I found them worthy enough. Get something fresh and we will work on you."

There was no limit to my happiness that day. I for sure knew that whatever he was talking about was not available in Mumbai; there is nothing fresh there, from journalism point of view. The city had been ripped apart to the level of being infertile for people who want to give something fresh.

Informing him about joining 'Sach' for some time I started getting into details of its immediate status. Everyone was busy with the Industrial Zone project, lot of PR articles were done by Neelu, to build the image of Pahargarh, and many of those articles were carried by *Times of Hindustan*.

In that time, I hardly met Neelu, except for work. I did not want to tell her about my new found love.

I moved back to MP to take charge of 'Sach'. A lot had happened there, by then. Television was to be launched, in about a years' time and the Industrial Zone project was just about to be full-fledged and functional.

First meeting with Keval after that incident did not give me bitter feeling anymore. In fact, I did not even remember what happened between us. As promised, we never spoke about it and I was given back my position.

Everything seemed happening and I did not miss those two eyes anymore. I was on a mission. We enjoyed our birthday week, Master and Neelu went on a Singapore visit for one full week.

Shivam Raj Singh, the MLA of Pahargarh was very happy with the Industrial Zone joint venture. He was quite impressed by Master's work and invited him to join his political party. But Master refused him for some reason. He said that he wanted to focus on his business, but actually his father did not want him to join politics.

As I rejoined, I got to know that Dr Bijoy Bhaobhi, who had returned to India, was Rajput's friend. A few people from 'Sach'; which is a newspaper with neutral political views, were actually giving the inside information to Bijoy's NGO, that was fighting for people's right?

This was something strange, I did not understand the purpose of it and there was no reason for me to support them. It wasn't even clear to me if Keval was aware about this.

As far as I was concerned, I played safe; posing as if I did not know anything, in my absence Dabbu was anyway taking care of 'Sach'. I was on my hunt for breaking news. To my surprise, I got something that had a deep connection with my best friend, Dabbu.

There was a student Karan Nagpal who was killed in college ragging by his senior Dharmesh. Karan was a rising star of the Bhopal cricket team and had a chance of getting into the Under 19 state team. Karan was coached by Dabbu's sports academy - Panacea.

Panacea was considered as the best sports academy of the state, and his students were trained by the national level coaches. Management and finance were looked after by his father while the approvals and other field jobs were done by him. Because of the exposure he received through 'Sach', Dabbu was able to build himself extremely strong.

A year before, one of his students, Junaid Ansari, was selected in National Level Under19 Cricket Team. It was for the first time in the history of the state that a player entered that team. He had the potential, and the Academy helped in grooming and training him.

Junaid was Karan Nagpal's idol and walking in his footsteps he wanted to get into the state team that year and two years down the line in the national team.

Karan was killed in the ragging. And his college senior Dharmesh was arrested. The senior had nothing against Karan, and the fight between them was not so intense. But since the evidence was against Dharmesh, nothing could be done.

There was nothing much in the story. All the newspapers had this as a headline–"A Junior Killed in College Ragging."

People believed story to the core. The whole parent fraternity was shocked, as something like this could happen even to their kids. All the parents with under-18 kids were worried and had voiced their concern about the incident in newspapers and television.

Everyone forgot the fact that this kid was supposed to get an entry in the state level team, and he was contesting against the famous builder Rishabh Khurana's son. Only one of the two could make an entry into the team and get special training from International Coach, Andy Ray.

I knew this was the story. Called up Shirish Sir and said, "Sir I have got it, I might be killed in the process but promise me if my story works well in 'Sach' you will cover it in your next Live Show."

I could feel him smile, "Sure Greshma and I know you will not be killed. My eyes are waiting for you."

It was not Dharmesh who would have ever gained anything by killing Karan Nagpal, and the next day front page of *Sach* read, 'So now Jeevan Khurana is all set to enter the State team, since his rival Karan is killed. A million-dollar guess for who is behind the murder?'

Media did its work; police got the hint and culprits were behind bars.

Shirish Sir was very happy and as promised he did take this issue up in his Live Show.'

*****

Chapter 16

Bundle of Joy

It cannot be an expensive ring

That brings joy, his mere presence could bring

To my bundle of joy, I would sing

The song called, 'fortune tiring'

Everyone returned by dinner time. They were impressed by the development of the place. It was named after Keval's grandfather, and they all had sweated their life to build that name.

In heart of hearts they failed to prove having any connection to the magnitude that the place possessed. They felt very small in front of the place.

At the entrance stood a big statue of Late Shri Keval Kishore Rajput, an old man who promised success and prosperity to investors in the project.

The place proved its promise; there was no factory which had ever shut down since inception, no labour problem, and every factory showed growth.

That place was blessed and anyone who got connected to it, prospered. The Scorpios were under the impression that it was their hard work. They felt like fools for having thought so.

"Guys are you aware that Late Pahargarh MLA Shivam Singh asked Keval to join politics immediately after the launch of this zone but he refused. Shivam Raj Singh challenged him, - *Iss zameen ka hokar tu na rehe sakega rajneeti se dur, ke hawaeen wapas lekar aayengi tujhe yahaan zaroor,*" said Raj.

"Ya, I know that, and after the launch of 'Sach National Television Channel', which was two and a half years after the Industrial Zone project, there was news that Shivam Raj Singh was serious. He had asked Keval to meet him, and finally succeeded in convincing him," said Greshma.

"Keval had learnt a lot about politics from him in those five years. This was totally against his father's wish, who hated Shivam Raj Singh for dragging Keval into the filth of politics," said Neelakshi.

"Shivam Raj Singh knew that he would soon die, and did not want his position to go to the local people. He made his deathbed a tool to emotionally blackmail Keval. He made Keval promise, that if anything happens to him, he would contest for the elections and also marry his daughter," said Greshma.

"What are you saying? I know some other story," said Raj.

"All other stories are wrong. This is the only reason behind his getting into politics. After his death, Shivam Raj Singh knew, there was no chance that his family would get the ticket. His daughter was very young so he could not even force her marriage to Keval, but this way he thought, both his objectives could be achieved," said Greshma confidently.

"Is that the reason why Shivam Singh used to get disturbed, when he would see me with Keval? And Keval used to get cranky enough to give me a reason to kill him. I thought so wrong of him. He could not marry me because he was caught in a web. He loved me, Gresh I was so wrong," said Neelakshi.

"He was playing with your emotions, you fool, he never introduced you to anyone, as your future wife, he never married you," screamed Greshma.

"He never married Shivam Singh's daughter either," said Neelakshi.

"You idiot, I don't know how to tell you, he was using you till Shivam Singh's daughter turned 18. She was just fifteen when he died. Even now there is one-year time for her to be of a marriageable age. He would have dumped you after a year from here, if all were alive. I know him more than you, Neelu," Greshma said with a heavy voice.

"Let's finish this daughter discussion here itself, please. Gresh I guess the opposition party was supported by Keval's cousins, who had equal stakes in Pahargarh," said Shashank.

"Yes, they were, but they could not do much. Master had won the elections with 8000 votes and had become the MLA of Pahargarh. From there began his hunger for power. In simple words I saw his true colours," said Greshma.

Raj did not want Neelakshi to get more emotional. There was a lot of torture that Raj himself had been through, after working with Keval.

Raj realized after a few years that the meeting with Susheel was planned and was a part of some game. They needed a person who was reliable, smart enough to do their work and *majboor* to follow their instruction without any apprehensions.

Keval knew Raj was the right person but to get him on track was not easy, greed was his weakness and Keval made full use of it.

Raj felt exploited when he got to know about the truth but, by then he had reached very far to say a word against them. Nor could he go back. He was a powerful puppet, powerful to the world and puppet at the core.

He controlled all his emotions, covered the anger in his voice and softly said, "Finish your dinner Neelu. Ok, tell me when are we going to Bhopal?"

Neelakshi replied; "Day after tomorrow, is a small *pooja* in the morning, after that we will leave."

"Is Maa Sahab also coming?" asked Greshma.

"No Gresh, she will be here for some more days and then will join back office. She has no clue about the working of 'Sach'. Gresh you would have to help her out." said Neelakshi.

"Then who will take care of Little Kishore?" asked Shark out of curiosity.

"He will be with me, he is my child," Neelakshi said firmly as if she wanted to send this message to Keval's Mother who was not present in the room.

"Relax Neels, let's go and sleep now, otherwise we might get into an argument. I just don't agree with your decisions, and I need to discuss a lot of things with you," said Greshma.

Rajat tried to make the situation lighter–

"Aarz kiya hai, nanha sa sheher jahan main palaa badha

Churata tha imali jahan tha pehera bada

Dost ko apne saath le jata tha zaroor

Pakda gaya to uspar ilzaam lagane ko ho jata tha majboor.

Par kabhi kiya nahi maine apne iss hunar par garoor."

"What nonsense!" said Greshma and ran after him to hit, because she understood what he meant.

All dispersed soon, as there was one more day with no action.

Greshma could not sleep; actually, none of them could sleep, but they did not want to be together at the same time.

Neelakshi was contemplating upon sending Little Kishore to India's best boarding school when he was eight, big enough to learn how to be with people. It was important.

One learns discipline when one is out of the comfort zone. But Maa Sahab was against this decision. Neelakshi could not take charge of her own son, and that hurt her a lot. Little Kishore was the only reason to live for both Neelakshi and Maa Sahab.

*****

Neelakshi thought of the time when she got to know that she was pregnant and not happy about it.

'Just after the successful launch of Industrial Zone project, Keval called me to inform that we got 25% booking in the first week itself. India was really growing. He sounded so happy that day; "Neelu my darling."

"Yes, Mr Keval Kishore Rajput, the rich man," I replied to him equally happy but posing that I was annoyed, I knew it was my efforts that paid off so well.

"Why are you getting angry? I was really busy and you know that. You had only organized that press conference and you know how it works. After that, there were meetings after meetings."

"Even I am busy Keval, there is no time for anything, but still I make sure that I handle your account personally. So that we could at least be together for some time."

"Okay, Okay, I have a plan."

"What plan?"

"We are going to Singapore for one full week."

"How can you plan my holiday? Do you even know my schedule?"

"Oops, sorry, so here it goes, Madam it will be really kind of you, if I could get one week out of your precious time as I need to plan a holiday trip."

"I would have to check my schedule," I replied in arrogance.

"Please, please Madam please," said Keval just to make me smile and I actually did.

"Okay, I can give you my time and it starts from Friday onwards," I said. I had my own PR agency by then and needed nobody's permission for a holiday.

"Great, then I will get the bookings done for Thursday night."

I never thought Keval could behave like this.

We spent a really good time together. And those few days were actually for me. Neither did he take any phone call nor checked any mails. Everything was awesome.

After we came back both of us got busy with work, far busier than before. Now Keval was not just a busy man, but a very, very busy man. He still did not forget his first Saturday meetings. I was instructed not to keep any press interviews on those days. Many times, I felt like asking him about it, but then there was no point as he would always do what he wanted to.

My visits to Bhopal and Pahargarh increased, and so did my PR agency's fee. I charged him heavily for the PR activities; after all, they gave good results. Meanwhile, I also got new clients.

The whole PR process was planned with the objective of image building in new markets and the plan delivered very well. My agency was paid three lakhs per month as a retainer fee.

One month after the holiday trip I realized that I was pregnant but there was no time for marriage. And even if there was, Keval felt no need for it. On one of my visits to Bhopal, he introduced me to Maa Sahab.

Maa Sahab liked me in the first meeting itself, but Dau Sahab had some other plans in mind. He wanted to get Keval married to his friend Dr Bijoy Bhaobhi's daughter.

For sure Keval did not love me, but it was very clear that he would not marry her either. I could never ever think of that Shivam Raj Singh's daughter, even in the wildest of my dreams. Keval had never mentioned anything about her. He did not want me to go for an abortion for some reason which only he had known. We decided that I would give birth to the baby secretly. My parents disowned me for this decision. It's been four years since I met my mother.

Eight months later, was born my bundle of joy during the winters of the pink city, Jaipur, in Maa Sahab's father's *haveli*. As soon as he was born, Keval adopted him legally as his son.

Thank God no one was able to guess about my pregnancy. I had taken off from work for two months, and everything was managed really well. In those nine months a lot happened on the work front.'

*****

As Neelakshi took a break from her thoughts, she heard someone knock on the door. When opened, she saw Little Kishore.

"Oh, my baby, where were you? I thought you were sleeping with Dadi Sahab," she said to the little one who was standing three feet below her eye level.

"No Neelu aunty, Dadi Saa snores, I can't sleep with her," said the little one who had been quiet for last two days.

"My god, I am so happy you spoke. Who brought you here?" she asked, hugged him and took him inside.

"Gresh aunty, she left me here and asked me to knock."

"You did not ask her to call for me baby?" Neelakshi kissed him on his cheeks, and rubbed her ear against them.

"No Neelu aunty, she said both of you are fighting."

Neelakshi smiled.

"Neelu Aunty, will you read me a story, like every time?"

"Which one do you want to hear?"

"Papa and Tiger story, the same one that you read out to me every time."

Neelakshi could not control her emotions and tears rolled down her eyes. She could not tell him that his papa was no more. And the tiger was never there. Her mobile started to ring as she controlled herself.

'Why is Bank calling me from the next room?' thought Neelakshi and picked up the phone.

"What happened, Bank? Why are you calling me from the next room?"

"I am just a messenger Neelu, Gresh wanted to know if you have taken Little Kishore inside. I could never understand both of you. You women are really strange."

"Give her the phone, Shashank," said Neelakshi. He gave her the phone, "Thanks Gresh, he is in."

"I am sorry, Neels, but I can't express what I feel for you. It's difficult to say."

"It's ok, sleep well, good night."

For Greshma Little Kishore was just like her own baby, he was just one year elder to her son Hridaan. Greshma was officially on leave when he was born.

She was with Neelakshi in Jaipur and had planned her wedding with Shashank, in such a way that everyone in the office was under the impression that she was on leave for the marriage. While her parents were told that she was in Mumbai on a project and would return back two days before marriage.

Greshma and Shashank had declared to their families that they would be bearing the expense of their wedding, and families would only come to give their blessings.

The wedding was unexpectedly elaborate. Since they were not sure of the date of his birth, a lot of permutation and combination were done.

If it was 28th December – they decided that it to be a simple temple wedding, if it was 29th December – they planned for a court wedding, if it was 30th December – they planned for an Arya Samaaj wedding, if it was 31st December then they decided to have Rajput style wedding and if it was 1st of January they decided to have a full 9 days Bengali wedding. And *janaab* came on 27th December itself, so they executed all the plans. It finally became a grand 15 days affair.

Chapter 17

Ups and Downs

When did life say it will be smooth?

It will take you through thorns and then soothe

It will give you a high and next moment low

Whether you keep pace with it or move slow

Life is life, it will continue to go

It was just not possible for Greshma to sleep. The whole discussion; secrets of Keval, Shirish, Shivam Raj Singh, and Dr Bijoy Bhaobhi were killing her from inside. She had seen the dark shades of everyone but was forced to be silent. Not everyone has the courage to come out strong, after being through what she had.

She re-lived the time again in her thoughts.

*****

'After tasting the first success and proving my worth as a potential star journalist with the 'Karan Nagpal murder case', I was very happy. My name was not brought to light initially, as Keval wanted to play safe with this easy, yet precious '*Mohra*'. But then there was nothing to feel bad about, I found my true love and had a good career.

Suddenly, one day I got to know that Papa had fixed my marriage date with Shashank and I was not in love with him anymore. He was to come to India soon. He had become very close to my family, despite of staying in another country, and even after staying with them, I had practically moved away from them mentally.

I just failed to understand why the horoscope game suddenly stopped. When, why and how did it turn in the favour of my parents? This was until Shashank opened the truth that he had convinced them.

I did not want to marry him, I wanted to be with my love and above all there was a contract which still had two years to serve.

Shashank agreed to the contract terms and was fine with my career decision as well. It was not easy to digest this side of him. He was always clear that he would never allow me to continue work, and would take me to the US immediately after marriage.

Everything about him had changed. A once upon a time Bank, who could make anyone slog to pay his money with interest, was not confident about his ability anymore. I was not able to understand the reason for his change.

A few days before marriage, I went to tell him what was going on in my mind, but when I saw him, I did not say anything.

As I looked at him, I felt the same touch of honest eyes. I felt so guilty for having done what I did. They were always there and I could not see them.

I went all over the world, slept with strange men in search of those honest looks with true love for me, and here was the man literally slogging for me, suffering for me to death, only to keep me happy and I believed in the story of Keval Kishore Rajput, that son of a bitch.

I agreed for marriage at that very moment, neither did I inform Shirish Sir nor did he bother to know. Our relation was based on a simple funda. If I was there for him, then he was there for me, and if I was out of sight, then I was out of his mind.

And for all the good reasons, I knew that no one could mess with my career. There was a lot that I knew for which they needed me.

The day Little Kishore was born, I left for my marriage. The very same day we got the news that Neelu's father had expired. I left her in grief, but there was no other option. I had already messed with my life enough and did not want to do that for Keval anymore. Neelu had taken a very wrong decision and as a friend I was with her till it did not affect my life. I was never in favour of her decisions.

It was as if uncle had come back in her life, as her son, to get answers to his questions. He was back to witness how she would repent for her decisions and make her realize that she was wrong. He could have been a chauvinist man, and a strict father, but he loved his daughter a lot. Neelu could never understand his love.

After two months of marriage, Shashank left for the US for work. I realized that I was pregnant, and it was his child. I was happy, but there was no time to rest. I knew that the luxury which Neelu had for her delivery was not meant for me.

In that nine months' time my son saw the dirtiest side of people, something a mother would never want her child to come across.

But my son is a special child. He is strong; he fought hard along with his mother for truth.

The deadline decided for the launch of 'Sach News Channel' extended to two years. Even the Newspaper 'Sach' was evolving under the guidance of Shirish Sir. The column 'Link up' was being used as a blackmail column.

Launching a National Television channel and sustaining it required a lot of money; I could see everyone running for it. My job was not doing that directly, but everything I did knowingly or unknowingly was being instrumental in the plan.

Somewhere I could see Keval becoming too dependent on Shirish Sir. Dabbu was getting close to Keval's father, and Keval just did not like it. Something strange was happening.

After a very long time Shirish Sir called me up, "Hey Greshma, how are you?"

"I am good Sir. How about you?"

"Not really good without you, my bed misses you and so do these two eyes. They are just waiting for you."

"Sir," I did not know what to say, I was married and pregnant, having found those two honest eyes for life.

"Sir please let me know the project for which you have called."

"Smart girl Greshma, you know how difficult such conversations are for me when I am at work," he said with a sigh of relief.

"Yes Sir, I know it and more over now I am married."

"Please don't give that crap Greshma. It's difficult to take such things from you."

"Sir, please may I know the purpose of this call?" I said sternly.

"Of course, Dr Bijoy will be giving you a list of fifty people with project titles."

"Is he the same Dr Bijoy who is close friends with the Rajputs?" I enquired.

"I don't keep his friendship records, Greshma, and I don't like any interruption when I talk."

"Sorry, Sir."

"There will be five people who would help you to source information about these fifty people. They will be from Dr Bijoy's NGO," he said and paused, which indicated that it was my turn to ask questions.

"Is there anything in specific that you would like to share Sir?"

"Just keep it to yourself, not much interaction required with those people and to settle your curiosity this information is for his book 'Kick Back' where he will be unmasking many criminals, who have a clean image in public. So, this is another big challenge for you."

"Sure Sir, I will take care," I said, and we got into the job. The whole work took around thirteen odd months to complete and in that process, I coordinated with Dr Bijoy as well. The list also had Shivam Raj Singh's name. He had a lot of skeletons in his cupboard but had a very clean image in public. When he got to know that he could be exposed, he got a heart attack and the only person whom he saw to his rescue was Keval.

He called for Keval immediately, so that he neither had to worry about his daughter nor his MLA seat. It would become a home affair, if everything went as planned. He even organised a few sessions of his daughter with Keval. Keval's life already was so complicated that those sessions did not affect him at all.

Shivam Singh died and Keval took over as the MLA of Pahargarh. In those two years many incidents coincided and they just kept me guessing.

Dabbu and I were getting very close as friends, I could never guess why. He helped me a lot during the project 'Kick Back'.

Mr Kishore Keval Rajput had started trusting Dabbu more than his own son, Keval. On the other hand, Keval was doing everything against his father's wish. Still, he did not stop his first Saturday visits.

It had become like a joke amongst us, the only reason that gave us little time to laugh. Everyone was seething from inside, but we never said anything to anyone. We were trapped; the strengths, of which we were once proud of, became a curse for us. He had manipulated everything for his ambitions.

The saying, 'Either have a dream or slog to fulfil somebody else's dream' was a well fit for us. We had talent, but it took us time to realise our dream.

Though we would joke, that there was one more woman in his life who stayed on that Indore-Dewas highway, but knew we were actually making a mockery of our own helplessness.

Neither did we know the secrets of his life, despite being with him for so many years, nor did we know how to take control of our lives from him. We used to communicate with each other in bits and pieces.

Once the project was over, 'Kick Back' research team suddenly went out of scene and even Dr Bijoy stopped interacting with me.

I got news from my reporters about some five people, who died mysteriously in five different parts of MP. They were instructed to not to pay attention to it. I thought of digging into it but did not, thinking that many people come and go in life, and you can't keep a track of everyone.

The book was launched through a publisher from London, as none of the Indian publishers were ready to get into any kind of controversy. I was not even invited for the launch.

When I bought the book, it was shocking to see that they exposed only 20 people and they too were not from the list which was given to me. I thought my work was not liked.

I tried speaking about it with Shirish Sir but he ignored and started avoiding me.

My contract was about to get over in six months' time. The News Channel 'Sach' was launched, just one week after the launch of the book, I could sense there was some connection between the two but could not figure out what.

I was allowed to host my first talk show, and it was a big hit. Shirish Sir left *Times of Hindustan* and joined 'Sach Media Group' as a Business Partner with 50% stake.

I guessed that was the game, for which they used me as a liquid property. The mystery of where he raised money from was still unrevealed. It is not easy to own a media house unless you have literally robbed crores of rupees from somewhere.

Kick Back received a lot of publicity through Neelu's PR agency. Shady in one of the episodes of 'The Rajat's' mentioned about *Kick*

Back and the NRI status of Dr Bhaobhi jokingly, but it did not affect Neelu's efforts. Keval agreed to join politics, even when he knew that his father was strictly against his decision.

There was so much happening that I did not understand which wire was connected where, but something was strange and I could sense it for sure. It was not the right time for me to form an opinion and bring unknown facts to people. So, I was quiet, focusing on easy assignments that led me to fame without taxing my brain.

By now we were 31 years of age, old enough and matured. Shashank had started becoming bald. When he came after almost two years of our marriage, I could not recognize him and funniest part was that Hridaan, our kid, refused to go to his father. By now he had become closer to Dabbu.

After becoming the MLA of Pahargarh, the aspirations of Keval grew higher. Before his death, Shivam Raj Singh had introduced him to path of 'the secret treasure'. And now his only aim was to become Chief Minister of the state.

Keval's father was totally against this decision; he knew how dangerous this decision could be, he was worried to the core. It was strange to see a successful businessman, who was capable enough to turn the table of the game, over-reacting to his son's progress. His becoming CM could have actually opened doors for many more business opportunities. But he was not ready to understand.

Keval's first step towards creating history began with a grand party in a seven-star resort in Mud Island. This party was graced by top businessmen, politicians and Socialists of the country. People were brought in by helicopter. Bollywood celebrities were invited to perform for the event. There was no limit to the fun and frolic.

The next day of the party we got to know that Shady was arrested for killing his wife,'

*****

Recalled Greshma and tried to sleep.

Chapter 18

The Truth of Life

The truth of life is plain

Fail you lose, win you gain

You might go thirsty when in rain

Without need you lead life in pain

Life works on one principle; you have to pay. The way it unfolds itself is amazing. We act and re-act to the challenges thrown to us without realizing that life was just playing with us.

Greshma could not sleep and woke up as Shashank's snoring disturbed her. She went to the sofa and thought of the old time again.

*****

'News of Shady's arrest shocked us all. He loved Kiran so much. I went to meet him in the Mumbai jail without informing anyone. He was not an ordinary person by then, and even I had taken my first step to fame as a media person and his friend of course. The police allowed me to meet him, after a lot of coaxing.

"Why did you kill Kiran, Shady?"

"Trust me, Gresh, I did not kill her. I wanted to call you all, but they did not allow me to. They said that they will arrange a lawyer for me and I can't choose one on my own."It was difficult to believe his words, "You are not able to get me to your side dude."

"Give me one reason why I would kill her. I can't even take a single step in life without her; just imagine how I will live without her. Trust me, I have not killed her Gresh," he pleaded before me. By now I could make out the difference between the culprit and the innocent.

"Ok, tell me exactly what happened, they will not give me too much of time."

"I will give you just one name, 'Dr Bijoy Bhaobhi', I don't know if you will believe me or not."

"What?"

"See, after his *Kick Back* was making rounds in the media; I wanted to know a little more about him. You know my presentation; I always share the inside stories, to make it more interesting. Whilst researching about him, my sources informed that they had got a hint of him having strong connections with the smuggling world."

"I can't believe it dude."

"You have to Gresh. They got to know, that I was digging into their secrets and could prove to be a danger to them any time. So, they trapped me."

"Why did they not kill you?"

"They did not kill me because I had already hosted that show. If that episode had not come on air, before they got to know that I was aware of his roots, they would have killed me. But they killed Kiran so that I could not escape. I can't talk to anyone. I don't know how you are allowed in despite being a media person."

"I don't know what I said, but they just allowed," I said and before we could go any further the time was over.

Next day I returned to Bhopal, whatever Shady said was disturbing me. He got to know that Dr Bijoy had connections with some smuggling group for many years. He was a world-famous Economist and a famous writer. Through his NGO, he was empowering people, and he plans to launch a book on corruption. When the book gets published, it has a totally different content. It was all very confusing for me to get to the roots.

I shared my doubts with Dabbu, but it seemed that he did not get the head or tail of what I was saying. After listening to the whole story, he just laughed at me and asked me to go home and not to go out anywhere.

He thought I was too stressed and dropped me home. He forced me to leave my car in the parking itself. But saving Shady's life was more important.

The only person whom I could next approach was Shirish Sir. He had practically shifted to 'Sach' office, and the biggest cabin on the first floor was given to him. His cabin was smaller than my cabin though, but he did not seem to have any complaint about it, I was just an employee. He was the owner.

This cabin was a little different from his old cabin; it opened to a sitting area and inside was a translucent wall which technically separated the two areas. Since there were curtains inside, you could not see anything from there unless they were moved.

Despite Dabbu's warning, I came out of the house and went straight into Shirish Sir's cabin. As I entered, I could hear him speaking on a loudspeaker. Probably he was working on the computer, so both his hands were busy.

The man from other side said, "Sorry Sir, she just mentioned your name and we thought you have sent her, so we let her meet Rajat Chandani. Otherwise he is not allowed to meet anyone."

"How much time did she spend there, you rascal?" asked Shirish Sir. "Only five minutes Sir," the other side said, and I realized they were talking about me.

"Just kill the bitch before she leaves Mumbai," shouted Shirish. I was standing right in front of the curtain wall.

I did not know what to do; if I stayed back, I would be killed.

I thanked that curtain wall and rushed out. Luckily, no one had noticed me in the office.

I called up Shashank, but he did not pick my phone. Master was least bothered about 'Sach', all he was interested in was his Chief Minister position. How he could let his dream project be taken over by criminals? 'That is why Keval's father doubted his abilities to handle business.' I thought.

I rushed to Dabbu; he was just about to leave from Bhopal for some meeting with a minister in Lucknow, and I said that I wanted to go along. It was safe with him.

Once he was through with his meeting, we decided to call Shashank there, along with Hridaan. Thankfully, he was in India. They came, and we decided to go to Ladakh from there. Such a drama, yet Dabbu could give us ideas to enjoy a holiday. As it is, we had hardly spent time as a family together.

Just before we were about to leave for our vacations and Dabbu was to leave for Bhopal, we saw the news on television that Shirish Sir died in a car accident. We were shocked, and I was relieved at the same time, but still going back was not safe. Drama in life was on its peak that time. The second in command of 'Sach Media Group' was absconding, and the man who ran the show was dead.

Stories were being circulated about his mysterious death, in a car accident and my sudden disappearance from the scene. There were always speculations about our relationship but I never cared. I was strong.

I enjoyed the trip and came back with a fresh perspective towards work. There were many questions raised, but they were all shirked off when people knew that I went on a family holiday. Very few people from the media world could believe that I was married and had a two-year-old kid. A good family frame always saves you from many raised eyebrows. I realized that.

I took complete charge of 'Sach' as there was no one to dictate to me anymore and everything was set for me. I used everything, I learnt from my mentor to come to limelight and rose to fame.

Now even my greed to own a Television channel increased. But I knew it would cost a bomb. Earning that money was not easy.

After Shirish Sir's death, suddenly Dr Bijoy Bhaobhi was out of focus but Shady's case was still on. He was released after one and a half years. We got to know that even Dr Bijoy Bhaobhi had died in a mysterious car accident during his visit to India.

Neelu took care of Shady's daughter, Diya, during the period when he was in jail. They became so close to each other, that Diya started calling her 'Maa' and Neelakshi started feeling like one. Her son never called her 'Maa', so she felt very nice.

The law of universe is strange; it gives you everything in bits and parts.

It's said that first you struggle discovering what you want. You get wings in this stage, even the universe supports you. In the next step you realize your true talent and nurture it, this time goes in learning and in making a strong foundation. You get exploited in this stage but you don't complain, you take it as an investment.

Once you cross that stage, your fight to earn respect begins. This fight is to satisfy your ego against the humiliation you faced in the previous stage.

The stage next to it is actual achievement. You don't mind taking any route to maintain this stage. You are still immature, and this immaturity is complemented with the arrogance in you. The third last stage is protecting everything that you have achieved. It's precious, and you can't stand anyone who exhibits himself as your competition. You fight to pull everyone down.

The stage next to it comes to very few. It is called satisfaction, where you enjoy everything you have.

The last stage is maturity; you reach to self-actualization and evolve as a person. Everything that you do in this stage takes you closer to *"Param Pita parmeshwar"*.

We are forced to reach this stage. Reasons are different for different people. For some it is loneliness, for some it is health problem, for someone else it could be another tragedy. It's basically because of our incapability, to understand the second last stage. Very few reach there after attaining satisfaction.

These stages are natural and they come in everybody's life depending upon their capability and aspirations.

We were all in a transition phase between stage three and stage four. It was difficult to control our emotions and actions.'

Thought Greshma as the clock showed 1:30 am, and she decided to sleep.

*****

7:30 am Gresh's cell phone rang. It was kept on the centre table, in front of the sofa. Shashank woke up disturbed. He saw the name, and it was Dabbu. He did not pick up the phone. She was still sleeping. One full ring, but nothing could disturb her.

Not that Shashank was worried about disturbing her, but it was Karan Kataria, the man who was a closer friend to his wife than him. It was jealousy that made him not pick the phone up.

"Keval slept with her and **that is why I wanted to kill Keval**, but I don't feel good when Dabbu calls her. I feel helpless when it comes to him," Shashank said to himself and her cell phone beeped again. Greshma woke up disturbed and picked up her phone. Shashank kept looking at her lost in his thoughts, "She is so beautiful, so young, and her lovely hair fell on her cheek making her look so innocent. When she runs her fingers through her hair, I feel like grabbing her into my arms. The way she gets up from her sleep, makes her look so fresh, so adorable, I feel like sleeping with her again. Her voice after sleep sounds so sexy. How could I be without her for so long? I want to have sex with her," he said to himself, went close to her, took the phone as she was about to say hello, disconnected it and switched it off.

"Morning love; I have not even brushed my teeth," she said. He looked at her with a mischievous smile, kissed her and went on, without saying a single word. It was after a long time they made love.

Chapter 19

The Co-passenger

Every journey has a station

Everyone is sent with a mission

Which one to choose is your decision

For success one needs a broad vision

Karan Kataria (Dabbu), the tall handsome man, had almost lost his charming smile. He was still regular with his gym, but his love for sports now changed into preparing sportsmen. His passion for travelling was now replaced by growing the tourism industry. He had won awards for his contribution in developing 'MP Tourism' and growing its revenue to three times. His third love of being with 'The Scorpios' was now replaced by 'Sach Political Party', ever since he joined Keval. He learnt a lot in that four years' time and his political background helped him even more to learn the tricks of the trade.

He used to think of Keval as his inspiration without realizing that the world started trusting him more than his inspiration.

Today he was sitting in a mess, with people calling him and bombarding with questions. He had answers to everything, but not the courage to say anything. Something from deep inside was stopping him from moving ahead. These tough years had turned him into someone else. Karan lost his mother to poverty, when he was very young; his father had to go through a lot of humiliation for taking the side of truth. They had nothing to eat when his father had to give up everything for politics.

The true essence of Politics was lost, and changed into a policy of changing policies and a money minting game by few selfish people. Mr Rajan Kataria (Karan's father) had fallen prey to these people. That is when he decided to give up politics, but even that decision of his could not bring back the mother of his kids.

He made a lot of efforts to get back to his normal life because he had to live for kids. Mr Kataria earned his respect and money back through his intelligence and hard work, but never returned to politics.

Karan lost his pregnant wife to politics, too. They met with an accident as part of a game plan, in which practically he was supposed to be killed.

He was a loser yet did not want to give up. He began to unfold his journey from when he was forced to join politics.

*****

'After winning that award, my whole life changed. Baba was proud of me and after years I had seen him smile. I promised myself, to make it stay put on his face forever, I would do whatever possible on earth. My full focus was on developing my sports and tourism business in the whole of MP at any cost. If it was tourism anywhere in MP, there has to be Karan Kataria.

If these guys had done wonders through their Industrial Zone project, even I was earning name and fame in my expert field. I heard during this time that Mr Shivam Raj Singh, the MLA of Pahargarh, had asked Master to join politics, but he refused, as his father was totally against this decision.

This was Shivam Raj Singh's revenge against Kishore Keval Rajput. Shivam Raj Singh had 'Brain Washed' Keval completely and after becoming his partner in the Industrial Zone project his expectations from Keval increased.

Mr Kishore Keval Rajput called me home to talk about something serious one day all of a sudden. This was after the successful completion of Industrial Zone project. He had not been a part of the project but knew about each and every detail, including the amount of wealth they were making and the means by which they were making it.

Master was not the one, who would keep all the money to himself. He always paid fair to his partners in crime.

"Karan, I need your help," said Mr Kishore Keval Rajput with a fear on his face.

I was taken aback, after listening to him and could say nothing but, "Sure Sir."

Mr Kishore Keval Rajput was a shrewd businessman; he grew his business in the era when it was not easy for players in his field to sustain. The market was ruled by big players, and the customers were few.

Mr Rajput not only grew the construction business started by his father, but also diversified into manufacturing of raw material required for construction. The manufacturing units were set up in the most accessible locations so that he could offer better price and have no competition in the towns that were seeing a construction boom.

This not just helped him become friends with competition but the business integration plan helped him to become a single solution provider. He was in good books of everyone; in the era when export was not an easy thing his mango export business did pretty good.

He was hard working but just hard work was not enough to raise money. There was something he had hidden in the dark and was the reason of his fear which was so blatantly visible on his face, that day. I wanted to know the reason but did not have the courage to ask. It was my first face-to-face meeting with him, so I did not intervene much. Politely I asked, "Sir, may I know what you expect me to do?"

"Karan, I want you to be with Keval," he said in a demanding tone, "and I will give you as much money as you need for your business, even more than what you could think of." A concerned father turned into a shrewd businessman and then into a devil.

Who would refuse such an offer, at least I wouldn't? My uncle and father were anyway taking charge of the administration work of both the sports academies and the tourism business was in collaboration with the government of the state. The time had now come to pump in money and I was already on the hunt for a source. Keval and his father's fights over proving his capability were famous amongst us, so I did not mind.

I accepted the job, and it turned out to be a thrilling game. It was an adventure which only real men get to perform. I went through turmoil, but never gave up.

As a part of the deal I was supposed to give all the information to Mr Kishore Keval Rajput and he would guide me on my action plans, but nowhere even by mistake was I allowed to mention about his involvement in this game.

My payments were made by Mr Rajput as announcements. A picture was created that he was supporting me in my business as an investor. For the whole world he was trying to help me in my career and I was portrayed as 'Keval's *chamcha*' on the other hand.

It was so difficult to understand both the father and son; they played games with me turn by turn.

That game is still on, even after the life clock of both Keval and his father has stopped. I am still struggling with the mess of minutes and seconds that they had trapped me in. There is a fortune river but full of crocodiles, I might get killed in the process. People call it greed, but for me to swim across it is passion. There is a thin line difference between the two. People say when aspirations exceed their limit, they become greed and when passion exceed its limit; it becomes hunger. Everything is labelled as cheap. Your sacrifice is taken as your ruthlessness and your commitment to what you call passion is taken as madness. The whole dictionary of words changes for you and also changes people's perception about you.

They start getting scared of you; they form a silent 'hate club', against you. They hate you because they don't have the courage to become you. They are helpless as much as you are. Their fear encourages you to go high, even higher towards your aspirations. You keep on achieving and achieving, and they keep on increasing their hatred towards you. Not everyone reaches where you are; it's a place reserved for only the select few. Then you rule.

Initially things weren't that difficult as my job was only to be with Keval and keep updating Mr Rajput about what his son was up to. He could have hired a private detective but the detective would have never been as idiot as his friend Dabbu.

Since most of his trips were between Delhi, Pahargarh and Bhopal, it was not that difficult. I could see him getting closer to Shivam Raj Singh. He used to teach him the basics of politics and open the secrets of his, 'All Friend Theory'. Even I used to visit Singh at times, rather most of the times since, it was a part of my job.

A few things that he said were easy to understand. Since my father had always shared his knowledge and experience about politics, just as a true politician, so I could connect easily with this world. I could make out the thin line difference between how it is and ideally how it should be, which Keval could not.

I was getting lakhs as sponsorship, for my academy from the biggest sports shoe brand. This was the first favour done by Mr Rajput in return for my services and I was happy.

One evening I was given a deadly project. The project was to kill five people, with two simple conditions. These dead bodies should not be found together and they should not be recognized. It was a task. Murder is something I had never thought of.

"Sir, please I can't do it," I said to Mr Rajput.

"Karan if you don't kill them, someone else will and then neither would you be able to get land for your third academy, nor would I be able to get my son."

"But that was not a part of our deal."

"There was no deal either. You kill and get paid; you don't kill and get nothing."

I slept over his proposal, but did not discuss about this with anyone, not even with papa. It was not a part of my father's philosophy.

The next morning, I agreed to Mr Kishore Keval Rajput's proposal. He promised to give all the support. I was not supposed to do anything except planning and supervising the execution.

The challenge was **time**. All five of them were to be killed in a single day, I was not supposed to go anywhere, but only instruct. A team of executers was allotted, and I was given a temporary SIM card for this project.

I was given photographs of all the five, these guys had never come across me in my life and I was planning their death. Planning is something I learnt from Keval and today I realize that I am better at it than him.

I made sure all their clothes and belongings were destroyed so that nothing supported their identification. Cops were a part of this game too, so there was not much problem. The strange part was that Mr Rajput who never believed in taking any sort of political and government favour had managed this game.

The man in photo 1 was killed by the man eaters of Jhabua. They left nothing but bones.

The man in photo 2 was thrown in the mouth of crocodiles of Bhedaghaat, Jabalpur. The man in photo 3 was burnt in a fake Hindu-Muslim riot.

The man in photo 4 was killed in a train accident. His body could not be recognized.

The man in photo 5 was killed in an acid factory, even his bones were destroyed.

I never wanted to do this work but to get the land, for the state's largest sports academy I thought it seemed like an easy project. After all, I was just obeying orders.

Only Gresh could understand my happiness. She is the only one with whom I could be happy in true sense, without thinking about the controversies, which go on in my conscious every second. I was never caught for murder and would never be; they were planned very well. Not even Gresh knows about these Dark Secrets. We were both like puppets in Rajput's hands.

Gresh was happy for me as I was progressing in my career; and even she was. I helped her unofficially in collecting the data for a very good project 'Kick Back'. It was supposed to be one of the biggest projects of her life. It had come in the market with a different data and all her hard work went down the drain.

She was upset but the book was a hit. She even mentioned about the team, that was helping her officially and after the project she was not in touch with anyone. I could understand her completely.

One evening when I was busy with a corporate football match in my academy Mr Rajput called. It was immediately after Shivam Raj Singh had a heart attack. Somewhere I was responsible for his heart attack. His name was there in the list of 'Kick Back' accused, and just before the book was to launch, I vaguely shared it with him. It seemed like he knew about it. He got scared, as his public and political image was clean, only he and the Rajput family knew his shades of dark.

Thankfully he was recovering, and I was a bit relieved. Mr Rajput had some fear. He got information that Shivam Raj Singh was planning to kill Keval and so he asked me to kill him.

"Why?" I asked and he got me an approval for a huge land, connecting *Kaliamba* dam on lease for my water sports activity. And 'The Why' became insignificant.

Shivam Raj Singh was killed in the hospital itself; doctors said that suddenly his health stopped supporting him and his heart failed.

Now I was getting busier with so many lands in my name. There was a huge task ahead, and my duty with Rajputs was on. After Shivam Singh's death, Mr Rajput thought that things would improve and he would get his son back, but to his surprise Keval decided to contest for the MLA elections. Mr Rajput had his first minor heart attack then; it was unbelievable; a father who was always complaining about his son's incapability was so dissatisfied with his son's success, that he got a heart attack. His tension got him to recovery in fifteen day's which usually is the other way round with normal people. For sure, he was a few of the rare cases born on earth.

After taking his responsibility as an MLA, began Master's big task of building a strong Political Empire. This Empire would get us majority in the elections. The battle to reach 'CM Chair' was two and a half years down the line. State elections were fixed and so were our plans of action.

'The Grand Party' as it is known, had all the who's who from politics and business circuit. I took charge of inviting the guests. It was a challenging task; I took guidance from Mr Kishore Keval Rajput backstage.

It was so difficult to convince Chiranjeev Shrivastavaji for the party. When he got to know that even his step brother Chirantan Shrivastava was coming he just refused the invitation. So, then the challenge was to choose the most important one and obviously the first one was far more important than, his useless stepbrother. As a polite gesture I sent police to raid Chirantan Shrivastava's illegal liquor factory and he was caught up for over a month. He had to pay a big price for just accepting an invitation.

Over 500 people graced the party, and it was one of the most unforgettable one, for years to come. Chefs were flown down from across the world so that guests could enjoy the authentic flavour. I hit 90% of my target, which was not a bad deal. The ones who did not turn up were in a majority from the business world, who probably did not have any agenda on their business card, to get off-the-record approvals.

Everyone enjoyed the party. Lot of deals were made along with new strategies, to further exploit the pockets of the common man, and the soft music added charm to their discussions. These strategies ranged from Re.1 to an indefinite amount. Just imagine the population of the country, even if it is a single rupee, it will not be less than minting minimum 100 crore a day, and excess has no limits

I realized that night 'Money is a magnet'; it gets attracted to only those who have it with them, or at least have an idea of how to route it towards them. I had an opportunity, to talk about my business, get some political favours - after all, I had won an award from the Ministry - but, I did not.

Awards go to people who have been kept away from the opportunity to make money. They are forced to maintain a clean image, used as a show piece and encashed, on their goodwill whenever required. In other words, they are taken for 'fools.

Now, here I am firm in my mind that I will walk on the path shown by Mr Kishore Keval Rajput to build money. The after mission was to strengthen the bond. We did this by personally meeting every guest, even if they could not make it to the party. Master gave the latest and most expensive model of Scorpio SUV as a token of appreciation.

The number plates had a similarity and despite not being a part of this party directly, media sniffed it out, and soon it became a rage amongst media people. Whenever they came across any of those Scorpios they would sarcastically mention, 'so you were also a part of that Grand Party it seems' and would proceed on their job with a vicious smile.

This buzz kept on making rounds for almost three months. It raised Keval's fame even higher. Neelakshi was given the assignment of involving media, without actually involving it and she did her job extremely well.

Next day when we came back, we got news that Shady was arrested for killing his wife. Gresh called me to discuss about a strange meeting she had with Shady. We got to know that Dr Bhaobhi had connections with smugglers. He killed Kiran and trapped Shady in it. The mystery was going beyond understanding.

Gresh was very upset; she could not even connect to her official 'Kick Back' team members, who were apparently assigned by Dr Bhaobhi. She showed me a photograph of her with five of them.

I did not have the courage to go back to the photographs of the five men, whom I had killed. If all official members of 'Kick Back' team were to be killed then even Gresh's life was in danger.

I did not pay much heed to her words because telling her more meant, getting her closer to the danger. I ignored her words and dropped her home. There were two bodyguards which I kept for her without informing her. Next morning when I was just about to leave for Lucknow for my PR meet, she came home worried. I knew the danger was now right in front of her. I took her along and asked Shashank also to join us there.

That was the time when I was enjoying limelight. The most important job in hand for 'Sach Party' was to do a courtesy visit to, Mishraji, MLA of Lucknow. He was a spiritually and mentally evolved person. Being a Politician by profession (though unofficial) and Brahmin by caste it was my moral duty to bond with him. I knew 'the grand party' didn't mean much to him, but for me he was an extremely important person. He was a man with power, and strong connections in MP. Having him in our favour meant, more MLAs by our side.

Mishraji deliberately kept the height of his entrance door low. He wanted anyone who entered his house to bow before the *Mandir* which was parallel to the door. He believed – "no matter how high success takes you, one can never be God, omnipresent and supreme" Even the Prime Minister, was to enter the same way if he ever came.

As I entered, he said, "*Katariaji Namaste, kaise aana hua?*"

"*Bass Mishraji, sorry itne, short notice par aa gaya.*"

"*Nahi ji aap hi ka ghar hai kabhi bhi aa sakte hain. Aur bataiye kaise hain?*"

"*Mishraji bass, apka ashirwaad hai. Hameen bhi kuch thoda bahut seva ka avsar dijiye.*"

"*Aree Karatiaji bass apka bolna hi bahut hai. Do shabd pyaar ke alawa aur kya chahiye. Waise loog apki dawaat ki bahut tareef kar rahe hain.*"

"*Bass ashirwaad hai apka, Chaliye ab chalte hain.*

Humko bhi yaad rakhiyega," I had to say this important line. Everything in politics is about marking one's presence.

This is a game of friendship; someone is always somebody's friend, if not yours. I knew Mishraji would support us by all means, if not upfront then definitely at the time of need.

After the meeting, I organized Gresh's family trip to Ladakh. She needed a break, and so did Shashank. He seemed to be going through a really rough phase.

The evening before I was about to leave for Bhopal, I received a call from Mr Rajput, after a long time.

"*Beta* Karan, Shirish is now a threat for Keval," said Mr Rajput. Taken aback, I said, "Why Sir? Why would he want to harm Keval, they've both been good friends? In fact, he has invested so much of his time, money and energy in his media house. Keval even agreed to give Shirish 50% partnership in his dream project. I know how much Keval loves 'Sach'. It's hard to believe that he wants to kill Keval."

I knew I said a little too much over phone but there was no other way to give him an indication that he can't talk nonsense and keep making me kill people for his own whims and fancies.

Dr Bhaobhi was after Shady's life; Mr Shirish was after Greshma and not after Keval's life. It seemed as if Mr Rajput was trying to fix some game for his son from the backstage. Somewhere something was wrong. I went on thinking, trying to connect the missing links.

But he threw a bone in front of me again, a 50% partnership in his IT project. Even if I sold that land, I could build my chain of hotels in Khajuraho, Pachmari, Jabalpur, Ujjain and Dewas. My mind stopped analysing, and without hesitation, I asked;

"What do I have to do, Sir?"

"Just kill Shirish."

One more murder. It was too much to do. Why I was made to do that job went beyond my understanding. I was not a *'supari killer'*, one whose business is to take life without emotions. But the role was similar. It was horrible, I felt like a woman, who was forced to take up prostitution.

I did not want to get into that state of mental helplessness for life. Unsuccessful in gathering the courage to share this feeling with Gresh, I lapsed the night drinking like a crazy with Shashank.

Gresh was surprised to see us together.

Next evening before departing for Bhopal, media broadcasted the news of a road accident which led to the sad demise of Mr Shirish, the famous journalist; ex-group editor of *The Times of Hindustan* and partner of country's fastest growing Media House, 'Sach'.

Throughout the footage, Keval was kept out of focus, as he was busy with his party's promotions. Meeting people and collecting money for election campaigning was his job. The Industrial Zone project was completely handled by a hired team that used to give him daily updates. There was no formal communication between father and son except for that call on every first Saturday of the month.

Now it became of utmost importance for me to know about that Dark Secret, the only link between those two sharp minds, even in this stressful time.

The speed with which 'Sach Party' was growing was like the first day abnormal returns for a listed company on a stock exchange, and I found myself playing an important role in its book building process. Mr Kishore Keval Rajput used to keep an extremely strong follow up with me. It accelerated to an extent that at one point of time there used to be only his name in my caller list.

I was growing leaps and bounds, doubled my speed of grasping things, and soon became the right hand of Keval and left hand of his father. I was minting with both the hands but somewhere there was no satisfaction.

Just eight months before the elections, there was a big fight between me and Keval on some issue. It became the headlines of media– 'Rajput-Kataria' split. I was no Minister or MLA; technically I was nothing but a '*Chamcha*', yet the focus was always on me. As if I was the diamond embedded on the crown. Rajput's did not mind that much; they used me like a dog.

Master's *Chaachaji* made use of this opportunity and came to meet me at my office. He looked quite similar to Mr Kishore Keval Rajput, but did not have a moustache. They say in a fight some forty years back, Mr Kishore Keval Rajput made him shave it off in front of the whole village and warned him not to keep it. He was caught stealing. *Chaachaji* never dared to keep it, but from then on there was a never-ending fire of revenge that had taken shape in his heart.

"Karan *Beta*."

"*Namaste Chaachaji*."

"*Beta*, I understand how it feels to be insulted and this father and son are famous for it. They will use you to the best of capacity and then throw you out of their lives as if you were never there."

"*Chaachaji*, I am not in a mood to say anything."

"Anyway, if you want revenge, then come to me, my doors are always open for you," he said and left.

I could not sleep the whole night, but did not go to him. The third day he called me and at once I went to meet him, without giving a second thought. *Chaachaji* was really sharp and had done all the ground work for destroying Keval's political career. He was unhappy with the Industrial Zone project, which according to him was on his land.

He introduced me to the opposition party members, who were faking to support Keval, but were plotted to back out at the last moment. He opened some secrets about the Rajputs, which even I was not aware of, this gave me a hint that I needed to be aware of them and all of them. It took me one and a half months to understand his game plan in depth and I realised – 'The most valuable commodity one has, is **information**.'

On the 46th day *Chaachaji* was arrested for killing a woman. She was a renowned actress of Bollywood some twenty years back. He was said to have a secret relation with her. With this arrest *Chaachaji's* career and family life were, totally destroyed and that was my objective.

It was my eighth murder and I went back as the same loyal left and right hand, of the Rajput father and son. Media headlines now said, 'Rajput Kataria resolve their mutual dispute' and I got more land parcels to build hotels and sports clubs, in all the top cities of the state.

There was hardly six months' time left for the election, and even I was very busy with my business work, and the party work. Keval's popularity was growing, and so was Mr Rajput's fear. His behaviour was beyond my understanding. One day he called me to inform that his friend Dr Bijoy Bhaobhi was in India, and he had come to kill Keval.

That day I reached the peak of my patience. I could empathize with those people who as per his father, wanted to kill Keval. It was not difficult for me to relate to the mental torture that the father-son must have been taking them through.

If the world wanted to kill Keval, then I was all set to kill his father. By now I was so close to Keval that could read his mind, count his pulse and plan his game. He was a different breed, but rare. His strong and weak sides were coming in front of me, layer by layer. It was as if I could see him naked.

But his father was always a mystery for me. I wanted to scream, but my voice was choked with two crores in Indian currency.

There was another car accident but in Delhi this time, that killed the Economist and Social worker, who brought laurels to the nation. His connections with the underworld never came to light. Dabbu was soon out, but in a mysterious way. He never ever spoke about Dr Bijoy, and the research report story.

By now I killed nine people; just two more were left to reach to auspicious eleven. The 'who next' fear kept on haunting me.

Soon everyone got so busy with the elections; a clean image was to be maintained. It seemed as if all the Rajput enemies were dead. Mr Rajput stopped calling Keval on every first Saturday of the month.

Father and son reconciled, and soon Mr Rajput started interfering in Keval's political decision. Not that he doubted his son's decision anymore, but now his objective was to get me out of the picture. I knew just too much for their well-being.

During this time, I got a confirmation, on Mr Rajput's involvement in my father's political career. *Chaachaji* had shared this with me, but I had deliberately ignored, thinking that he was conspiring to brain wash me against the Rajputs.

Finally, the D-day arrived and results were out. None of the parties could get majority in the house.

It was now time to play the Friendship Trump Card. Majority of MLAs were by our side. The ones who could not openly support were paid enough to decide a reason for their absence in the session with the governor. That job was totally mine, and I did it at the cost of my wealth.

In these elections I lost everything, including my pregnant wife. I was a broke, yet on duty.

The meeting started, and this '*Chamcha*' turned criminal, stood outside the Governor House with all the extras, praying for the party wins.

Master used his charm in front of the governor.

"Sir none of the parties could get the majority, not even the big ones. I have the support of 95 MLAs, and this makes me eligible to form the majority in the house. I request you to give me a chance once."

He was very young, yet all the MLAs supported him, biggest reason was his clean image. The perception was that if he would not do anything good for anyone, he would not harm anyone either and they could keep on playing their game without worry. Two-and-a-half-year campaign played a big role in building his positive image. India is a young nation and a young person should be given a chance.

To build his clean image all the dirty work was done by Karan Kataria, the son of a man who sacrificed his happiness to keep up the integrity of national politics. Mr Rajput used me and all that was a drama, created by father and son. They won and I lost. I was just a shuttle cock in the game.

Finally, Governor *Sahab* agreed, and our government was formed, no his government was formed and I clapped for destroying my own life.

Keval Kishore Rajput was the youngest Chief Minister of the state at the age of 33 years. Of course, I was jealous of him.'

*****

His face turned red in anger thinking of all the calculative games played against him in last four years' time. He had lost more until he realized all that he had gained. He tried calling Greshma again. She finally picked up the phone.

Chapter 20

The Ray of Hope

When dark covers the blue

Mind dwells to see something new

It's hope that survives in hearts of few

All have their own personal view.

"Gresh, what happened to your phone?"

"Nothing Dabbu, my battery went off and then we all went down for breakfast."

"Just shut up Gresh, you are not on an island; you could have taken Bank's phone. I am dying here and you are trying to please that bastard Shashank."

"Dabbu please yaar, relax. I am sorry."

"I hate your being with that man. You lose your mind when you are with him."

"Please, for God's sake, Dabbu talk sense. He is my husband. Tell me what happened?"

"Gresh, I will be taking the Chief Minister's position for this five-year tenure." Gresh screams loudly, "What are you saying, you idiot? Are you mad? Do you even know what it means? Oh God, oh God, oh God! I just can't believe it. It means we are not finished."

"Calm down, Gresh. You can't scream like this. It doesn't look good. You are still in Keval's house."

"Don't worry, Dabbs, there is no one around, and I will control my emotions. Ok, tell me the whole thing."

"Since we were already in majority, we have the power, and I have convinced others as well to support us. The crab story works very well in politics and above all everyone knows me."

"So, when are you to take the oath?"

"The news is not made public yet, meeting with Governor Sahab is today and only then will everything be declared."

"Don't worry dude, you will definitely succeed; I always knew you are more capable than Keval in every way."

"Let's see, Gresh."

"Does that mean our money is safe?" asked Greshma in a soft voice.

"Yes darling, the money is safe and in six months to one year's time, we will be able to see our dreams taking their shape."

"I am so much looking forward to it, Dabbs."

"Just finish the formalities and all of you come here. Five-year plans are already set, but to get our money we need to still be very thick. This world is full of opportunists, you slip a little and these crocodiles are just waiting for you, with their mouth open wide.

Other than the IT projects, there will be one more Industrial Zone which will be approved, and this one will be the largest in India.

MP being a state that connects all the four parts of the country, we have worked out an extensive road development project, and metro project, to facilitate trade through sea, from Surat Port to Indore. We have other proposals like educational institutes, student's banks, etc., which are to be considered."

"Wow; that is too much. You know, Dabbu, we are always with you. We will make sure we are back by tomorrow evening, *pooja* will be early morning. After so many years I could smile without any burden in my heart."

"Great, see you then tomorrow evening."

Greshma was happy; it was the day; she was waiting for. Things seem to be happening. 'It will not be a dream anymore. My dream will see the light of the day' she said to herself.

Shashank was with everyone in the dining room having breakfast. They were all then to work on the next day's *shanti pooja*.

It was clear from their faces that the *Badi Haveli* seemed like a jail to everyone now. It was no more than a place of action, but they did not want to show it to Maa Sahab. They all started taking official calls and replying to mails. There is no life without work.

Seeing those faces, Greshma just wanted to break the big news, but she stayed quiet, though everyone could notice a change in her behaviour. She was talking positively now and was not wanting to dig into the past anymore. If at all anyone tried to bring her back, she would just shrug and move on. She seemed to be shining like a diamond in the coal mine.

By evening the news was confirmed, and they all collected to discuss it quietly in her room.

"Guys, we got to get going now. Tomorrow early in the morning after the 5:00 am *pooja* we have to leave. I have arranged for cars, and all five of us are going together, including Neelu. Luggage would be kept in the other car," said Greshma.

"Have you gone mad Gresh? I am not coming with you all, I need to be here for some more time and Maa Sahab needs someone to be with her," said Neelakshi."You are mad Neelu; please get over this Maa Sahab fever. When she has already made plans for her life, why are you stopping yourself for no reason? And if you are worried about Little Kishore, you just tell her that you will be leaving him, and then see her reaction," said Greshma.

"What do you mean, Gresh?"

"Neelu, you just see. Every single drop of blood that pumps her heart makes her think more practical. She is a woman with a practical heart and you are an emotional fool who lives in pretence."

"Don't get into that again, Gresh. I have asked you to stay away."

"You might feel I am cruel, but I know that I am right, Neelu. After Shirish's death, I realized what being practical is, and it's only after that I grew to such heights ruthlessly."

"Please stop your cat fight here. Just imagine we will all see our dreams come true now. Neelu will be able to expand her PR agency to international level with her own offices, Gresh and my dream of having our own media house will now take shape, Shark's dream of having his own group of Industries is just a night away, Shashank's dream of having his own investment company is not very far," said Rajat.

"I thought people are supporting Thapar, or Pandit, never thought our Dabbu would steal the show, *waise haque banta hai yaar!*" exclaimed Raj, and suddenly the graveyard turned into a celebration lounge.

"It's really hard to believe, I thought people will take back their support, given to Sach. Media never took Dabbu's name even once. In fact, Sach was almost written off," said Rajat.

"What else do we want? Its news to die for," said Shashank.

"Smart plans work, and this is politics. It changes in minutes and seconds. But please hold your horses' guys. We are still in Maa Sahab's house and there are strange things that are going on. I know she is keeping a tab on us, because she feels we are the only ones whom she could use as her life support," said Greshma.

"I will not give into this woman; we have surrendered enough to the Rajputs. Anyway, just for your information police is suspecting a murder plan against Keval and investigation has already started," said Neelakshi.

"Let's live once and leave rest to destiny. We have died enough," said Rajat.

"So, let's just be quiet till we meet next, tomorrow morning at 4:00 am, finish *pooja* and leave by 7:00am, so that we can reach Bhopal before the day ends. I am sure we will not be able to reach for his oath ceremony, but at least we will be able to discuss our next plan of action," said Raj.

Next day, as per plan, they finished *pooja* and left Maa Sahab with her grandson and a bunch of servants in the *Badi Haveli*. They were 15 minutes before the scheduled time. Greshma had arranged for the latest model of Scorpio for all five of them. She decided to not to keep any driver, so that they had enough space to discuss.

As they crossed 80 kilometres from Pahargarh, they came to the spot where their friend had met his destiny and left them for life. All could hear him scream from the valley but ignored. They moved on, without even looking back. They had already paid enough and were determined not to look in the past; today no Master could use them for friendship's sake.

While they were on the way Mr Karan Kataria was declared, as the new Chief Minister of the State, he was even a day younger, than the last declared CM Keval Kishore Rajput. He was all set to take the pledge and sign the documents.

As he occupied the chair a vicious smile covered his face which was very different from his usual smile. Many congratulations and welcome messages greeted him, but he was waiting for some special people. The day was busy but he wanted to be alone. He sat for a little while with his father and then went into his cabin, instructing guards that no one should disturb him for some time. Alone he sat in his cabin,

*****

'Thanks, Keval Kishore Rajput. If not for you and your father I would have never understood, this mystery of life. You said friendship, I said friendship. Your father said deal, I said deal. But you and your father both said distrust, so I said distrust too.

The game can never be one sided and no one is weak. It's all the war of mind, the one who has it, wins. Your father made me kill those five people without giving a reason. He understood my weakness and I did his and yours.

Those five people were to be killed because they knew the secret behind the launch of 'Kick Back'. Your father was friends with both Mr Shirish and Dr Bijoy. Shirish was given 50% partnership in 'Sach' but to raise his share of money was not an easy job.

After all, there is a limit to the amount of money that an employee can put in, so he took help from Dr Bijoy. For the launch of this book, a list of corrupt people was made with the description of their Dark secrets. These rich people were then blackmailed and were forced to fund money that helped Shirish in claiming partnership in 'Sach Media Group'. This money was painted white and routed in through the right channel.

Some people were given signals of their secret love affairs, through 'Link up' section of 'Sach Newspaper' and that was enough for them to dig the hidden money, out of their forefather's grave and do their bit of contribution, to the 'support Shirish cause'.

The book had to be launched and it did. The beauty of the book was that all the shortlisted names were removed from it and there were obvious names, which already existed in the public domain. Mass did accept the book with open arms. At that time, you were deliberately kept busy with politics and other work. Your father was good at chess and knew how to change people's role to save the king. He was a *wazeer* playing the game.

I knew Gresh's life was in danger, so I sent her out of focus.

The *wazeer* of the game asked me to kill Shirish, saying that he wanted to kill you, when the fact was that poor Shirish had become a danger to Rajput's stake, in 'Sach'. He raised money beyond expectations and became over ambitious, wanting to bid for the full stake instead of 50% partnership. So, your life's name killed your good friend.

Shivam Raj Singh was a waste for your father anyway. After he got to know that his scams were mentioned in 'Kick Back', he got a heart attack and decided to use you against your father. He blackmailed him about bringing to public notice the secret of your highway farmhouse. The secret that made your father what he was. I was asked to kill him. I knew the secret that you had kept in the heart, all your life, the secret of first Saturday.

Your father was a bastard of category one. During the days when growing business was not easy, he agreed to grow weed in huge quantity in his sugarcane farms on your land, in the outskirts. You went there every first Saturday of the month to deliver the stock and collect money.

These were foreign parties who had warned your father, to not to get into any political or government issues. They extended all the support required by him to grow his business. He had no option, but to involve you in the business. After him it was only you to take charge. But you hated it. I still remember your cynical behaviour when we smoke. I caught your weakness. Even Shark knew the secret but you played such a mind game that he could never come out of it.

Those people could have killed you and your father, so the only option left with your father was to use me to kill all of them. You were planning against us ever since we left college. You were there at every step to make sure that we were fully instrumental in your plans. You became our Master, I know you hated me, the day I shared how 'Charas' was made. But you did not say a word.

You had a good platform and connections along with the capability, but you needed people to execute, so that you were free to think and maintain a clean image. Even till today there could be nothing proved against your father.

Rajput's were blessed by *Maa Durga,* but nowhere in history has anyone ever written about victory of a demon. You were one.

You built your economic strength using Shark, you built your media strength using Gresh, you built your image by using Neelu, you built your international contacts using Bank, you built your social image using Shady and you built your political image using me. Yes, you had first built your empire to build yourself. Every role was so defined; it took me so long to understand.

You decided to join politics and your father knew that once you win the elections, no one would be able to reach you, not even the smuggler friends of your father. He tried to cover you from every side to the extent that he publicly broke the relation with you.

This secret was known to both your *Chaachaji* and Shivam Raj Singh, and that became the reason for your father to cut all the connections with them. He was not even interested in the Industrial Zone project, but who could dare to stop you?

Dr Bijoy was a man with two face. He was a part of the smuggling gang, his face as an Economist was only to get into the good books of people. He was seconding the smugglers' gang. When Shady got to know about his truth he decided to kill Shady, but that would have only brought Bijoy into the focus, so he got his wife killed.

Shady's life was not important for your father. When Dr Bijoy had come to India just a few months before the elections he had an argument with your father. Your father was growing weak, but he wanted to save you. Bijoy's life was not important, nor was ours, but yours was. He had planned your wedding with Dr Bijoy's daughter to save your life, but somehow it did not materialize. Bijoy warned your father, that he would kill you and so I was asked to kill him.

I did not believe in the stories against your father, told by *Chaachaji*. But you both started plotting against me. Your father forced me to give my land parcels to the MLAs, so that they vote in your favour. He convinced me by saying that it would be treated as a bribe if the Rajput's gave them directly. He had already made the transfer papers, to my surprise. These were the same parcels which I earned while killing those nine people.

I had already started my projects on those lands. But the cunning man had no mercy for anyone; I was no more of any use to him. When I warned him that I will expose all his secrets, he plotted for my murder, but in that accident, I lost my pregnant wife. Not just that, he was the man who spoilt my father's political career, twenty-seven years back and made us go through a hell of a life. I lost my mother because of him.

In those days when my father got to know that some rich people were helping foreigners in drug smuggling from our city, he started his investigation. But your father plotted against papa much before he could reach him and got him into the wrong charges of bribery. We had to leave everything; we had come on the road. My mother lost her life because she did not get medical aid on time.

You won the election and reached on top of the world, but I could not even express my anger against the man who made me a lose everything.

Your father took away everything I earned. If the means were wrong, then I had already paid the price, but both of you were still to pay. I did not want to kill you, but there was no other option left. If you were dead, he would automatically die.

Now don't blame me for it Keval Kishore Rajput. Everything happened with the consent of *Maa Durga*. She could have saved you if she wanted to. She did that once long ago, and that is why, instead of playing some dirty game like your father, I encouraged you to seek blessings from her after the victory, leaving you with no other option but to accept.

Your father hated me for it. I wanted justice not from you or him, but from her. There was nothing left with me to fear about losing, by all means it was my fair turn to win. This time the whole universe joined me in conspiring against you.

I played the role of a friend till the end Keval; I gave you signal to win at every step that night. But you were in your own world of arrogance.

Acharyaji's words were the first message to you; you could not see the helplessness in his eyes. He knew you would die.

Barman's decision of sitting in car 3 was the second hint; he never used to leave you alone, not even with your father, let alone me. But you did not question him even once.

Van accident on the way was the third hint, you could have decided to stop and check if there was anyone inside. There was no soul in the van and with your orders Car No.6 was free from your duty, to take charge of my duty till you were dead.

The driver gave you fourth hint, but you thought he is just too talkative.

The horn communication between the drivers of the truck and your car was another indication that something was wrong, but you ignored it completely.

There are many *dhabhas* on the road, but Barman called you just before the second one and the *dhabhawala* was another signal, unfortunately you did not pay attention to his words.

The bullock cart old man was the seventh hint, he played with the brakes of your car, but you did not even notice.

The same truck came back to accomplish the mission, car no.1 swiftly moved away but you could not, there was something else decided for you. I wanted your last journey to be full of adventure, but you left the game much before I could play all my cards. Keval I had mastered your game, the game that both you and your father played with us. It was so easy to kill you. The philosophy of friendship worked, and everyone supported me, including your own Maa Durga.

Your father made me kill nine people; he never thought it would come upon him one day. He was helpless as much as I was. He used me to his full capacity, to save you but in the end failed. To complete the auspicious number eleven, I needed two more, so I decided both of you on my own. And now I rule the game that you started.

I have no regrets, Keval. This moment was designed for me by God how could you have taken it. This is destiny. I thought all the other Scorpios were also involved against me, so I continued the mind game by plotting to trap them in your murder and sent police to investigate, sent a message through your old mobile number, gave insights about their life to media. But Keval, they have equally been through the same harassment that I have, and I can't punish them for your mistakes. It is the time that even they feel alive and not puppets anymore.

We wore a confident face and had many achievements to our credit, but only we knew we were trapped and were victims to a mind game.

Dadaji told me once that *Karma* decides our destiny and it always follows us. God transforms the result of good *Karma* into the steps of success ladder, and that of bad karma to the size of a small pointed stone, and plays a game with us.

We can travel anywhere in the world, but we cannot escape from the effect of it. One day or the other, we have to step on either one of them. They would either lead us to glory or hurt us.

If you are smart enough to escape the effect of negative Karma, doors to heaven automatically opens for you. God has given you brain and being a Brahmin I am blessed with using this theory to the best of my interest. I strongly believe in it,' said Karan to himself and smiled.

*****

By evening they met their friend Karan Kataria, the newly appointed CM of the state and their partner in crime. They were content, as their hard work did not go to waste. It was after years that they smiled.

They drafted the new strategy and defined their roles to the utmost precision, leaving no scope for failure, and without wasting any time got into the execution stage. They had White dreams complimented with a dangerous Dark path, but they finally succeeded in their mission.

Chapter 21

The Price to be Paid

Aspirations have no limitation

Karma builds the foundation

Whether or not you believe in reincarnation

Life takes you to your destination

Time flew and all the friends created wealth, they parted to fulfil their dreams and decided to never meet again.

Four years down the line, Dabbu proved himself as the best Chief Minister ever in the state. State prospered and so did he. His positive Karma seemed so strong, that the result of negative karma diluted with time. It was clear that people wanted him as their CM again. But every second of his life he feared of stepping onto that stone of negative Karma. He never went to Pahargarh ever again and decided to be alone all his life.

Greshma and Shashank shifted to the US. She was partner in a leading news channel, and Shashank was on the board of Directors, with quite a few good investment companies. He had his own financial consultancy firm as well. They lost their son Hridaan in a road accident but yes now were staying together under the same roof passionately focusing on their careers without even talking to each other. Neelakshi moved to Dubai initially, she started her office there and it was doing well. Little Kishore was with her and Maa Sahab expired two years back. She visited India in every three months, to check the progress of Rajput Empire. But life is not easy alone; she married Rajat and shifted to London, where he owned his own entertainment channel. Diya, Rajat's daughter from Kiran, was very fond of Neelakshi and even Little Kishore needed a father. Getting married remained as the most apt option and they decided to give shape to their life together. They soon realized that it was not the right decision but did not have the courage to move out it, for the sake of kids.

Raj was heading the South Asian Industrial Association, and now had his own group of industries. His wife eloped with her boyfriend and never contacted Raj. No woman gave him peace in life. His kids were now studying in hostel and he had taken up spiritualism for mental peace.

Land of Pahargarh had bound them together and money had set them apart, not only from each other but also from their own self. Their aspirations had no limits but happiness has. The outcomes of Karma just wait for us to step on, in their most justified form and we effortlessly succumb to them when the time comes.